The Shadow
Behind the Dream

Phyllistone Termine

A Molding Messengers Publication

For information about permission to reproduce selections from this book, Write to Molding Messengers, LLC 1728 NE Miami Gardens Dr, Suite #111, North Miami Beach, FL, 33179 or email Info.Staff@MoldingMessengers.com

Library of Congress Control Number: 2020918446

Print   ISBN: 978-0-578-68237-2
eBook ISBN: 978-0-578-77078-9

A Molding Messengers Publication

The Shadow
Behind the Dream

Phyllistone Termine

A Molding Messengers Publication

ACKNOWLEDGEMENTS

Firstly, I would like to acknowledge my Higher Power for giving me the courage and strength to complete this.

I also want to recognize Mr. Elie for encouraging me every step of the way. Every time you saw me writing, you told me not to stop, but to keep going. If it were not for you, I would not have such a great accomplishment under my belt. Calvis Robinson, aka Starfire Galaxy, I confided in you with all my story's ideas; you never once turned me down, but instead gave me motivation. I am grateful for all you have done for me.

To my wonderful family, I truly appreciate you for all the love and support you have shown me since the day I was born. A special thanks to Michelle Termine, my lovely older sister; you have done a lot for me over the years, and none of your sacrifices goes unnoticed. I love you with all my heart, and the same goes for all of my family; much love. To my brother, Timothy Charles; I am taking this moment to express my gratitude: Thank you for every single thing you have done for me. You stepped up even when you didn't have to. The goodness of your heart shone a light on me when I was at a dark spot. I am forever grateful to have you as a friend in my life. Your loyalty will never be questioned.

Julio and Devonte, I am also giving you both a moment of recognition for being my best friends since childhood; I love you guys. I have learned a lot from you guys, and I will always remember that.

Getting to Know the Author

I am Phyllistone Termine, born and raised in Miami, Florida. My parents are immigrants from the beautiful but very poor island of Haiti. I am the last of four children. I have two sisters - Phyltrows and Michelle; I have one brother - Lionelson, who is named after my father, Lionel. My sister, Michelle is named after my mother, Micheline, and I am named after my oldest sister, Phyltrows.

I am currently serving a 54-month sentence in federal prison. I was convicted at the age of 19 on fraud charges. I also began to compose this book at the age of 19. I am a recovering drug addict; I have done all types of drugs and I have done all types of crime to support my habits.

Luckily for me, I came to prison. I caught myself before the effects of drug abuse and a criminal lifestyle ended my life.

I am a poet, songwriter, rapper, author, producer, and most importantly, I am a voice for all the people that have a story similar to mine. It is never too late to turn your life around. I robbed, sold dope, swiped people's credit cards, and almost lost my life several times. I dropped out of school in the ninth grade due to my gang ties. I was in the streets heavy since I was 14. Now I'm focusing on being the best person I can be and becoming a productive member of society.

Chapter 1

How do you cope with the fact that the person you love is with someone else? How do you live in a world where people are hateful? How do you live in a country where the people who built it are being oppressed? What is liberty? What is democracy? A mockery of the people? Innocent until proven guilty? Or guilty until proven innocent?

My name is Jamari Picand, and I ask myself these questions all the time. Life is so hard for me to understand. I am constantly on a quest for purpose and meaning. Life as a young black man in America in the year 2017 is difficult. Everything is so confusing to me. How did Donald Trump become our president if everything he represents is the opposite of what our country represents?

Clearly, this is not the Land of the Free but *the Land of the Oppressed*, where the rulers or head government officials are outlaws. This is the land where righteous die in vain and all acts of righteousness are political. Every deed done by the government pertains to its obsession with global economic control. The values and morals that this country outwardly expresses to stand for is a disguise to hide the wolf in sheep's clothing. We have known from the start that the leaders of this society do not respect our race or our people. The only difference between now and the 1700s is that guns are not drawn to our face, but to our backs. Our persecutors are the ones they place in our communities to protect and serve the people. Racism is the pestilence that has been destroying the world for centuries, infecting our children and killing our fathers. Still, there is no cure for this disease of an educated society.

The death of Trayvon Martin is a very tragic case that traumatized me as a young African American. His death lets us know that as long as you are a black man in this country, your life has no value in the eyes of the government. A man named George Zimmerman, who went on to beat the murder case by Florida's Stand Your Ground Law, gunned down Trayvon. He claimed he was protecting his life, but the boy was running away from the man and had an Arizona Iced Tea can and a bag of Skittles candy. The young man was of no harm at all and he lost his life because of a racist bigot who went on to auction the gun he killed Trayvon with for about 138 thousand dollars. The selling and purchase of that firearm is a complete mockery of the judicial system and the entire black community. The person who bought the gun is a racist who wants to own a gun that an innocent black guy was killed with. I would also like to add that the same man who murdered this young man also had another case for attempted murder. This violent white man should have already been put in prison, but no, the system lets men of white skin color be above the law. Like, the great Martin Luther King said, "Injustice anywhere is a threat to justice everywhere."

The reason I bring this up is that when I wake up in the morning and get ready for school, I have thoughts of fear while I'm getting dressed. I was born in Miami, Florida and now, I live in Williston, North Dakota. The crime rate in the small town I live in is not very high, but I am one of the thirty colored people that live here. This place is so country-like; the people here wear these cowboy boots and ride big trucks.

I have to walk to school in the snow and walk back home because I am poor. The scary part of this process is, what if the police pull me over and shove me or harass me because I'm black? Most of the time, I am one, if not the only, of the few people who walk in the street, and to long-time residents, I may even seem like a suspect.

At school, I'm always treated like an outcast, and the number of colored people that attend the school could be counted on the fingers of one hand.

Honestly, the biggest reason why I am in fear for my life is that one day, this kid named John in my world history class walks up to me and was like, "Hey man, I think you're cool. I don't know why my dad hates black people. We talk, and I don't have any problem with you and you're actually the first black person I've met." From that moment on, I knew undoubtedly that there are people who hate me just because of my skin color. It's kind of sad to even think that there are people who have hatred for a whole race of people for no apparent reason; and that's why I'm constantly in fear in this *redneck town.*

I live with my older sister and her husband and two children. The husband is also one of the people that is trying to sabotage me; I have to watch out for him - he's a sneaky bastard; I love my two nephews though; if only they knew about the cruel world we live in. When I think about it, how did a child who is young and harmless learn to have so much hatred for another human? Surely, those racists must have learned such behavior, because there is no way someone could have been born like that.

In Miami, my school had whites, blacks, Hispanics, brown skins, dark skins, and all kinds of people there. Nobody in school despised one another based on skin color. The Miami Shores police once stopped a group of friends and me while walking in the neighborhood in which we lived. The officers searched us and drilled us with all types of questions like, where were we going, what was our address, and many other questions, just for walking in a group. I was already used to these types of situations in Miami. The most hateful thing I heard was from a police officer that day; he said, "We don't like your kind in our neighborhood." The most confusing thing about that statement was the fact that we all lived within two miles from where we were stopped. That was our neighborhood as well.

Racism is confusing, but I understand it; people hate you for no reason and treat you differently because of the color of your skin. I often think about Miami, the warm weather, and all the different types of people. Williston is 95% white, 3% Indian, and 2% others- blacks and Hispanics. It snows 8 out of 12 months through the year and everyone knows everybody in this small town. One thing happens today, and the next day, everyone already knows what had happened. This place sucks, and I left the love of my life behind.

Her name is Carmena Belle. This girl is the most beautiful, interesting, intelligent, funny person in the world. She is one year older than I am, and she already graduated high school. Carmena is enrolled in college; this was her first year in college, and I was in my senior year of high school. I met her because I had all honors classes, so I ended up in a class filled with sophomores when I was a freshman; I will not ever forget this. In my Geometry class in the third week of school, we were assigned to the same group project and we became good friends ever since then. She never treated me like an underclassman. She was the sweetest person in the world to me. I am pretty sure that's why I fell in love with her; a simple man can't really understand the greatness of such a smart, sweet, but strong young lady. Carmena has the potential to be a modern-day Wonder Woman. Once she is committed to something, she stands her ground for that purpose. I love every single thing about her, even the fact that she has a mustache that's a little thicker than mine, and sometimes she's a bit too passionate about social media. She's always thinking that I'm messaging other females or some girl is posting a statement about me. Other than that, she is the most wonderful woman on earth.

I think it's messed up just how much your parents can mess your life up, even though they wish you the best. My parents shipped me off into the middle of nowhere to live with my sister because I got arrested by a racist police officer who profiled me because of the color of my skin and my hairstyle. I have dreadlocks, so they thought I was the one who robbed an old lady at gunpoint, and to make matters worse, my parents believed I could have done it too. The charges were dropped against me because I'm a juvenile and an honor student. The second time I was arrested was because I got into a fight with this kid.

The fight started because he was with a group of boys and I was walking with Carmena, and they start hissing and making all kinds of noises. We all know how most groups of boys behave when they see a beautiful lady walking by. Then this one guy, who I later found out was Mike Dagger, the nephew of some big-time drug dealer in the city, walks up to Carmena and says, "Why are you vibing with this gook? You should be out with a real nigga." After that, he pulls out a wad of cash and smiles widely so she could see his mouth full of gold teeth. At that moment, I don't know what to do, so I kept walking and left her behind. When I turned around, I saw her slap the gold teeth out of his mouth and his money scattered everywhere. I ran towards her to defend her because I felt this thug was going to try to harm her. Mike then pulls out a knife so long it could pass as a sword, I ran towards him and I socked him with all my power as he was doing this. He fell and the knife flew out of his hand into the street. All this happened in front of a corner store that is known for drug and gang-related activity. Some groups of men were laughing, some were drinking beer, and some others were smoking cigarettes, but everyone is completely hysterical.

In that moment, everything went silent for me. I grabbed the knife from the ground, and when I looked at the group of men, they started running. I initially thought they were running from me, then I heard sirens and then a cop spoke through a megaphone, he said, "Put the weapon down!" I complied with his orders and got on the ground next to Mike, who was still knocked out with blood gushing from his forehead.

In this moment, all I could hear was Carmena yelling and screaming, "He didn't do anything! That's not his knife, that's the other boy's knife!" When I looked up, she was crying. Her face was super red and she had snot in her nose. Even in that moment, all I could think about was how beautiful she looks. Even in pain, she still resembled an angel.

I was charged with assault, robbery, and possession of a deadly weapon. Carmena had to walk home by herself. She told my parents what happened and they picked me up from the Juvenile Detention Center. These charges were also dropped, but my parents insisted that I leave Carmena alone. They also thought I was in a gang, which is ridiculous. I am an honor student and my only friend is my girlfriend as I'm socially challenged, this means I have a hard time communicating with people. My parents thought I was going through a phase. I was arrested twice in one week for robbery, so it had to be true; I was robbing people. This caused a rift between my parents and me. How could they even believe I was a criminal? I stay at home all day and read books. I win awards every year for good grades and perfect attendance. All of a sudden, I am a gangster!

That goes to show you how even your loved ones don't really want to see you make it. After all of those events, my parents decided that they wouldn't lose me to the streets and sent me to North Dakota to live with my sister. The worst part of it was, I didn't have a formal chance to say anything to Carmena; it was winter break. They withdrew me from school without my knowledge and showed up to my bedroom door with suitcases and Greyhound tickets. They said we were going to visit them for the break. That was not even a problem for me since I missed my nephews, Jovan, and Marvin.

Two weeks out of town was nothing, so I told Carmena I would be back before school started. Then we got there and four days before school started, my parents left in the middle of the night without telling me anything. I woke up that morning, and asked my sister Jamesha, "Where's mom and dad?" She said they went back home and I was now living with her to avoid my death in the streets. I was so saddened by the level of deceit and trickery that had been committed by the people I was supposed to trust. I had nothing to say; I went into my nephew's bedroom and wept bitterly as I looked out the window.

Looking at the barren wasteland called North Dakota was depressing. On December 29, it was snowing heavily outside; snow isn't really fun. You know how you'd see kids in their winter coats and snow boots, having snowball fights and making snow angels in the movies; this was not the case in Williston, North Dakota. Even on a summer day, you would not see any child playing outside. This town was like a place where only people of age could have fun. I still haven't seen the joy on people's faces unless it was at the State Park, where all the young people went to have fun only during the summer.

I cried every day for a month until I got used to being an outcast. Imagine being from a big city like Miami and then moving to a small town in the very cold North Dakota. Everyone told me I sounded weird and I had an accent. This was like torture to me being so far away from my love who could be in the arms of someone else. We always keep in touch through video calls. Seeing her face would make my day but it would also make me sad because all the guys my age don't give a fuck about love.

There is a slogan in Miami - *M.O.B.* or *Never Trust a B*. You know I was always different from the general population. I just wonder if there is something that I don't really know about women that only makes you want to be with them for short periods. That's still a mystery to me. It may have something to do with sex. From what I hear, once you have sex with a woman, when you're done and you ejaculate, as a man, you get this feeling of depreciation that makes you want to leave; I wouldn't know because Carmena and I haven't had sex - we are both virgins. We are waiting until we get married to do everything traditionally. From what I have heard from guys in school over the years, sex is very enjoyable. They say that women who have been with many guys aren't the ideal type of female you want to with because sex with them isn't very pleasing. The reason why Carmena and I haven't had sex is that I'm scared I won't satisfy her. In my opinion, my penis isn't that big, and I don't want her to be upset with me because I'm not big enough. All the guys say if you have a little pattywacker, then your girl will leave you in search of a bigger one.

I love Carmena so much and I don't want to lose her because of my physical incapabilities. Thinking about her is a bittersweet type thing. It refreshes my mind, but I feel like my heart is being poked at with a stick. The same way a little kid might see a dead dog and poke it with a stick out of curiosity. This world is confusing. I get mixed signals from everyone. One minute my parents are proud of me and they love me. The next moment, they can't trust me and they are ashamed of me. The same thing with girls. One moment they are so sweet and beautiful and within the blink of an eye, they turn into this vicious predatory creature.

Life is so strange to me but this is all I know, so living shouldn't seem foreign to me. I also wonder why death seems more ordinary to me maybe because in Miami I am more constantly aware of my mortality. Ever since Jamal, my younger brother died, I began to look at life differently. I started to observe my life as a scientist would examine a germ through a microscope; looking at every detail without rest. Sometimes I feel his death was my fault. What type of older brother doesn't watch over his little brother? Jamal was 12 when he died and I was 14. His death is the reason why I study so hard because I want to make up for my mistake. Jamal and I were playing video games at home while our parents were at work like regular kids do. Then, after 2 hours of me whipping his butt in the game, he gets tired and says, "Jamari, let's go play outside." I ignored him because I was so into the game. The next thing I hear is a car smash on its brakes and the sound of a crash, followed by police sirens. You know the regular stuff that happens in my neighborhood. The crash sounded close so I decided to go outside and take a look. I will never forget what I saw that day, 7-12-2014. The police had their guns drawn on the suspects while calling for backup on their walkie-talkies. The neighbors were all outside watching, then my heart started pounding and I felt a cold chill go through my whole body and I started to tremble but I didn't know why.

While I was looking at this car that crashed into the back of another car while being chased by the police, I looked on the street and I saw my brother's shoes. His good shoes. The ones mom bought us for school that year. Immediately I saw that, I ran straight into our home, yelling my brother's name. "Jamal! Jamal, where are ya?" I got no response, so I went back to the front of the house. By now tears had already fallen over my face.

When the neighbors came to me and asked where my parents were, that was when I knew it was real. At that moment, I was speechless. I just shut down and walked across the street to see the accident from the other side. There he was, my baby brother Jamal, with one shoe on his feet, looking lifeless as he lay on the ground. His white tee shirt was stained with blood.

The policemen were shouting at me to back away from his body but I was deaf at that moment; I couldn't hear anything. I walked up to him slowly, unable to process the reality of the situation. When I got close enough to his body to grab him, my neighbor grabbed me and picked me up and put me inside his house. Mr. Pierre didn't want me to see him like that but it was too late.

By the time my parents were notified of what happened to my brother, he was dead. They said he died upon impact. The car was going so fast when it hit the back of the other car and the car spun out and hit my brother. The force was so hard, his heart stopped.

The next time I saw my brother after that was at his funeral. Seeing my little brother's body like that in the casket traumatized me but it also taught me a valuable lesson. As my mom would say, "The Lord giveth and the Lord taketh away." The lesson I was taught at that age was one that I could have learned later when I was older but I'm grateful to know the value of life at such a young age. That goes to show that death doesn't have an age preference, skin color, hair type, or gender. The grim reaper is the only white man that isn't racist.

My mom has been overprotective of me ever since and she tried to tell me it wasn't my fault but if I had put the video game down and joined him outside, he wouldn't have died and we both would be here in North Dakota, laughing at these country white folk. Seriously, Jamal's death could have been avoided but as for the guy that killed him, he should be in prison for the rest of his life. I think that's what makes everything more heartbreaking and confusing. How do you let a man get away scot-free for fleeing, evading, and committing a vehicular homicide? These cops tried to pull over Jacob O'Brien for not stopping at a stop sign. From there he put them on a chase. His license was suspended three times over and he was a habitual offender. This guy hit my baby brother with his car and killed him and only did 6 months in jail followed by 2 years probation. That right there is a mockery of the justice system but at the same time, Jacob is a white man and we all know white people get shorter sentences. Had Jacob been a black man, he would have done at least 5 years in prison before he would be eligible for parole. These types of decisions by the government leave its people in bewilderment. There are so many things that just aren't right but you know, life isn't fair; life is life. You must always play the cards you've been dealt, even if your opponent has seen your cards. I believe in fate but I also believe in free will, meaning the outcome of your life is determined by the work you put in.

Today is February 3, 2017. I just got home to one of the worst days of my life. This morning was going well as usual. I got prepared for school, gathered all my stuff needed for class, placed them in my bookbag, and took off. While on my way to school, I passed by the skate park where I see the goth kids smoking cigarettes before school. Everything was going fine. I got my phone in my hand, scrolling through my timeline on my blog, then I stopped by the gas station to buy some gummy worms. While I was at the register paying for my items, the cashier says, "Don't you play with me, boy. I have seen what you have done. Empty your pockets."

I responded, "What are you talking about?"

"I'm gonna call the police. Empty your pockets."

I emptied my pockets. All I had was a number 2 pencil and 5 dollars for lunch. Then the merchant says, "I'm sorry kid. You never know nowadays."

I stormed out of the store, too embarrassed to even pay for the candy, so I left. I'm not going to put money in those slave owner's descendant's pockets was what I told myself. I was the only black person in the store and I was the only one told to empty my pockets. Racism is so stupid to me. How could a person treat someone differently just because of the color of their skin?

The way I was treated this morning was a reminder that I'm a black guy in America. As a child growing up in South Florida, you are constantly told by your teachers that all odds are stacked against you. The system is made to see minorities lose and if you go to jail, you always have a way to go right back. They say you'll miss out on certain opportunities just because you're black. This is what you're taught in school as a young black man in America; that no matter what, you'll always have an enemy because of your skin.

Barrack Obama was the President of this country. The highest paying job, the most prestigious job our government has to offer was given to a black man.

That is real inspiration. To know that one of my brethren defeated fate in an everlasting battle to deprive our people of political, industrial, and emotional success. Barrack is the reason why Martin Luther King's death was not in vain. Destiny has no choice but to overturn its decision on making my people suffer.

The incident at the store was just another example of why our country needs to grow. After I left the store, I headed to school. Instead of walking in the street, I decided to take the alleyway because it was the fastest route to school. When I turned into the alley, I saw two white boys that go to my school. They were smoking a cigarette and smoking a Mountain Dew. They both had camouflage jackets on which Duck Dynasty was written with blue jeans and cowboy boots which had the confederate flag on them. I started walking slowly in their direction but not on the same side of the alley as them. I looked up at them and they give me this menacing look, so I smiled and looked back down. The first kid goes, "What's this nigga smiling about?" Then the other one slaps him on the shoulder and tells him to chill.

I made it to school after those two encounters, and I became paranoid, thinking that everyone was against me. I walked into my first class of the day, English. Upon my arrival, the whole class looks at me weird. That's normal though, stare at the black guy as he sits down. The bell rings and the teacher gets up and says good morning to the class. Then she gives us our assignment. While we were reading the story she assigned to us, she made a student read aloud while the others read in their minds. Then she calls on me to read, so I read what I had to and stopped. The teacher always chooses me to read every class, as if she is amazed at the fact that I know how to read. While I was reading, I felt as if I could read the other kids' minds. One kid would say, "Why is the retard reading?" or "He knows how to read. Amazing." These are the thoughts that run through my head. I felt like their thoughts were all insults and they were like spears being thrown at me, only to pierce my skin with ease. I was being hunted and slaughtered mentally. After English, I left for the study hall. So now I have time to process what happened to me this morning. I concluded that this is the normal life for a black man and shrugged it off. It was nothing to me by now. After leaving the study hall, I went to my world history class. Since we are in February, it's black history month and we all have to be taught about our country and its gruesome past. For me, this was another reminder of my racist encounter that morning. The professor started by making us open our history books and turning to page 367. Here lies an article about Dr. Martin Luther King and the Civil Rights Movement. She explained to us that he lost his life for the equality of blacks. Then one kid shouts out, "Why do we have to learn about this? We're not black! Once he said that, all eyes shifted on me and I began to sweat from being uncomfortable. His words were the words that represented what most of the class felt but also represented the social ignorance of the most delicate topic of America's history. Once those words left his mouth, the radar on my submarine started blinking red because I knew an enemy was nearby. The professor explained to him that this is an essential part of the country's history and we must be taught this so something like this won't occur again.

A girl slapped the boy who said the statement and told him that wasn't nice. He replied he didn't care and I couldn't beat him up. That was true. He is the best wrestler in the wrestling team and on the basketball team, and he is very tall. Although I can't hurt him physically, I wanted to scold him for being ignorant of the history of the country he loves.

At the same time, what do you expect from a Donald Trump supporter? That class was the most intense thing I ever went through. I also felt like I let my race down for not defending them publicly. As a black person, that is an unspoken law if someone is disrespecting our people, you must defend them. During moments like this, I wonder what would Dr. King do? I know I made the right decision by not fighting him. Fighting would have labeled me violent and all black people the same. I also felt like I should have told him that people like him are the reason why progress is so difficult because they aren't aware of the past which enables us to move forward. I wonder how many people have been in a spot where someone does something racist or says something racist but instead of doing what was expected of them, they shrugged it off. It takes a lot of strength to not respond in a non-civilized manner.

After class, John walked up to me and said, "That was fucked up, what Parker said." I told him simply, "It is like that sometimes." After our brief convo, he walked away. Now it was time for lunch, the most awkward part of the day. From not knowing where to sit and wanting to be alone; lunch is very weird. I sit at a table by the vending machine by myself. People always invite me to sit with them but I always decline because making a conversation is weird. During lunch, I just go on social media and see what people are up to back home.

The black kids invited me to their table, so I go sit with them and everything was cool, except that in my opinion, they sounded white. I know that's messed up because people don't have a particular way they sound based on skin color. We do relate though, because we share a common background and a common situation, being black in an all-white school. Kerry was from Chicago and she says that our hometowns are both drama-oriented and very dangerous. She is also very short and pretty. Quan is from Georgia and his family moved out here for a better life and because his father died, they needed help paying bills. Keylina is from Idaho. She's Mexican and it is absolutely adorable. She has a black woman persona. These are my only friends. Although we are cool, I still stayed a distance away from them.

Another thing that's wrong with me is that I'm shy. I'm what some people may call "scared of people." Once I get to know you, then we cool but I will almost never take the first step in any relationship. If I become fond of you, then you have a charm and an alluring personality or I don't fear your rejection. That's one of my biggest fears, being humiliated and rejected. This is why I don't put myself in those situations.

Anyways, so we were all at the table talking and stuff, then some kid walks up to our table and says to Keylina, "Go back to Mexico!" She ignored him but I immediately took offense to that because one, she's an American citizen; and two, she's the nicest person on earth. At that moment, my radar went off again but this time red dots were everywhere. By now, we were talking about how disrespectful that was and how racist this country folk are, and then another kid came to our table and dropped off a note. The note read, "y'all should kill yourself and make America great again." This was the final straw. I asked for the boy who sent the note. To my surprise, it was the same idiots from this morning. They sat at a table to the left of the cafeteria door, looking at us, laughing. I suggested we get up and leave. We left the cafeteria, which turned into a racial warzone filled with propaganda. I didn't tell the gang what happened this morning, so they wouldn't get worried about my safety.

The bell rings and we all separate to go to class. On my way to class, I see these two clowns again. I tried not to stare at them but they were looking at me sternly. Then they both walk past me and said, "Make America great again." I called them hillbillies under my breath and kept walking to class. When I walked into my Spanish class, the professor told me the principal wanted me in his office. I made my way to his office, not knowing what to expect. I entered the office and saw the principal sitting behind his desk like Mr. Burns from the Simpsons. He turns around suspensefully. "I been waiting for you," he said. I replied, "Yes, I know but I don't know why." Then he says, "I got a tip from someone. They said they saw you smoking early this morning." I replied, "No sir, not me. I don't smoke." Then he said, "Are you sure?"; and I replied, "Yes, I'm sure." Then he searched my stuff and found nothing, so he sent me back to class.

Chapter 2

Everything was confusing to me. Why would someone say they saw me smoking? I don't even smoke. Maybe someone is out to get me. Maybe it was those hillbillies. By the time I got to class, it was over. The bell rang, and now it was time to go home.

On my way out of the school, I pass by the gym area and bought a Powerade from the vending machine, then I walked out of the building. In front of the school, you see all types of cars and trucks. You can also see all the less fortunate kids walking home in the snow. I zipped up my jacket and braced myself against the wind and started walking home in the snow. My sister's boyfriend is supposed to pick me up from school but he always comes late for some reason. I feel like he does it on purpose. That guy has some type of abhorrent feelings towards me for some reason, and I don't understand why. Maybe it's because my sister treats me better than him. Whatever his issue is, I don't care. I'm not going to take rides from someone who hates me on the low. I'd rather walk.

I was walking home and then a truck with the biggest tires pulls up beside me, and they lower the window. Then the cowboy who has been harassing me all day says, "Go back to Africa, nigga," and throws his drink in my face. That totally caught me off-guard. When I saw his face, I already knew something bad was about to happen. Now that he threw a drink on me, it's game on. A war had officially started but the thing is, how do I combat my opponent? I know for sure that I'm smarter than he is but he can get his redneck friends and stomp me out. This conflict between whites and blacks is centuries old but for some reason, someone will always insist on fighting a battle that has no merit. Some people have no purpose and being racist gives them a real reason to live. As sad as that may be, it's true.

How long shall this madness continue? Surely the creator of the universe didn't put my race on the earth to be second to these white people. Surely my people can overcome anything. My people were not made to be bottom feeders and labeled violent and incompetent.

Anyways, that was how my day went. Now I'm just trying to get some sleep. I should call Carmena and tell her how my day went but I don't want her to get worried. She can be overly passionate at times. I just want to go home. I won't have to deal with this back home.

People there do the most racist stuff behind your back but over here in Redneckville, they are straight up with it. Today was very humiliating: I was accused of stealing by a store clerk. I got a drink thrown in my face, and white people are calling me nigga like it's the 1990'. I feel like Chris in Everybody Hates Chris, the sitcom by Chris Rock. This is unbelievable. I don't have anyone to talk to about this and I ain't no snitch.

Last night was mad crazy. This dream I had must be a sign from God. Things are about to get out of hand in this town. Maybe I'm just stressed out from all these racist B.S. I'm not going to school today, I can't deal with this. I'll just say I was sick. That's a damn shame, Jamari. You've had perfect attendance since pre-k and you're going to mess up your perfect record for these cowboy bums that can't even read. You know what? Fuck it, I am going to school and I am going to enjoy my day as if nothing happened. That's more like it. I can't let these people take away my joy, that's all I have in this cold world. My dreams almost always come true, though.

This world just might come to an end with all these hate for no reason and hate between religious groups.

What should I wear today? Should I throw on my Nikes or wear my boots? I'll just put the boots on. They will save me from slipping and falling in the snow. Did I have homework for English? Nah, I don't think so.

Walking through the hallways on my way to class was a little bit weird today. Everything seemed so depressing, it just had that feeling. Something has to be up with me. Every day in this place is saddening but grief is in the air like the smell of fireworks on the 4th of July. The people who usually walk around fearlessly, with their noses up, now have their heads down like they have been publicly shamed. Uncanny, but whenever I get a feeling, it's always true. When I got to my English class, I didn't feel the normal piercing looks when I wanted to sit. Today it seems like everyone is minding their business. I opened up my English textbook, then the bell rang. The teacher stood up, went to the dry erase board, then said, "Good morning, class. I know you all are sad about what happened to Chase and Zack but take this as a lesson and learn from their mistakes. We as teachers and parents always say drugs are bad and don't drink and drive. What happened to Chase is a prime example of why you shouldn't operate a vehicle under the influence. This is so sad, he was so young. For someone to die at age 19 really makes you wonder what does your own life has in store for you. I'm 37 and I have seen people die, go to prison. Friends come and go. Most of your high school friends won't be there for you ten years from now. I just want you all to learn from his mistake. Life is short, that's why you must make the most out of it positively. Chase wasn't my best student but he wasn't a bad kid, he was just misguided. My condolence goes out to his family and Zack's family. Zack is lucky to be alive as well. The car they were in was totaled but Zack only left with a minor head injury. My prayers go out to their family and friends. Anyways class, I know you all are mourning the death of your friend but we have a lesson plan to follow and we are behind so crack open your textbooks!"

When the professor was speaking, the only thing I could think was that must have been what I felt in the air. Her words confirmed what I was feeling. The only thing is, I don't know who Chase is and by the looks of it, everyone must really care for him. That's sad, to lose your life in a drinking and driving accident. His parents must be devastated. I know my parents were when my little brother died. I don't know this guy but I can feel the pain of his family. The whole class and I were not really focused, thinking about Jamal and the fact that life is so short, and you could die at any moment was really messing with me. English class seemed to only last for 10 minutes. The time was moving fast like we were in another dimension.

Once we left the class, it was as if we entered another dimension, similar to the one we just left, just bigger. The whole time when I was in the hallways, all I could hear were short pieces of people's conversations as they pass by, speaking about what happened to that Chase guy. We live in a small town, somehow of course his story would spread around like an airborne disease. When I think about it, it makes me wonder, what if I passed away? Would I get the same treatment? Would my death make such an impact upon the student body? Most likely not. Nobody gives a shit about me. I'm black; I could die right now and no one would care. I'm black, so they won't feel for me. They would just speak about me for a day or two, then it would be like I never existed. That's why I have to graduate and go back home before a tragedy happens to me over here and no one knows because some redneck buries me in his yard with the rest of the people he murdered.

Every class had that gloomy feeling to it, that's why I'm so happy it's lunchtime so I could talk to my friends. I know they will be in a good mood, they always are. Damn, I just remembered those cowboys might harass us today like they did last time. Something has to be done about this. Honestly, I can't walk around with that much pressure on me.

When I stepped in the cafeteria, everything looked normal except when I looked to my left, where the girls who play sports sit, (A.K.A. the sports whore table), I saw Connie Harris crying with a group of people surrounding her to provide comfort for her. I'm guessing she was dating Chase but then again, she was dating everyone, Literally. She dated almost all of the guys at our school. Rumor has it she got her first STD in middle school. They also say she already had 3 abortions. Women like her make me sick. Honestly, Connie is a very attractive young lady but she doesn't know how much she's worth. Right now, there probably is a guy who would love her to death but she would rather fool around with these guys that lure her with kisses and after, kick her to the curb like a stray dog. That's just a shame to me, how tarnished her name is. I wish her the best of luck. Maybe she will find someone that will love her even though she's a slut. There's always a guy that tries to turn a wild animal into a domesticated one.

I went to the ling to get my lunch and I also bought chocolate milk. The cashier looked at me like, of course, the black guy buys chocolate milk. I pay her no mind; I'm used to the fuckery that goes on. I made my way to the table and greeted my pals. Now that I'm seated, I looked across the room to see if the rednecks were there but their table was inhabited by some goth kids. After that, I opened my milk and took a sip. For some reason, I wasn't in the mood to eat. I supposed it has something to do with the fact that death is in the air.

I'm sitting across from Keylina and she is just so gorgeous. Sometimes I catch myself staring at her. It would be awkward if she caught me daydreaming about her, so I try not to seem attracted to her. Quan finally makes his way over and now that the squad is complete, we begin talking about Chase and how he died. I asked Kerry who Chase was and she said he was the one who sent the note yesterday.

When Keylina heard what she said, "Thank God he killed himself before I did. He was such a jerk." We all agreed that he was a jerk.

Then Quan said, "That's still messed up, the way he died though." We all also came to the conclusion he didn't deserve to die even though he was a bully. They also said his story was on the news and when they said that, it reminded me of my dream. So, I said, "Hey guys, I had this dark fantasy of a dream last night. I want you guys to tell me what you think the dream means."

At that moment it occurred to me that, in a way, I knew that Chase died. I dreamt that I was driving a car at high speed with an insanely wide smile on my face because I saw a car in front of me and I was going to collide with it at high speed. The other car had no idea about what was going on. I was going at it full force and when I got close, all I heard was the car horn. Right before we hit, everything went white and I saw news reporters and journalists with cameras and microphones in my face like I'm a politician. One reporter asked me why I did it and I was just looking confused because I didn't know what was going on. Then a woman snapped a photo and the flash blinded me. When I looked up this time, I didn't see anyone next to me and my hands were covered with blood, with the snow around me. That was when I started to panic. Every step I took was like I'm stepping on a cherry snow cone. I began to make my way home or something, I don't know. That was when the police arrived and told me to put my hands up but when I did, they still fired at me. That was when I woke up.

"Whoa. That's deep, bro," Quan said.

Then Keylina said, "In the spirit world, you're having a battle." "What do you mean, having a battle?" I replied.

"Well, my grandma told me, when you have a dream that involves blood, that means your spirit is seeking vengeance against someone who may have harmed you in a past life," Keylina said.

Kerry stayed quiet. She looked shocked by this conversation. I told Keylina that may be true because when I went back to sleep I had another weird dream.

I was like a king in Africa in the old days. I was covered in gold, sitting on a throne, and before me was 3 white guys bowing in front of me, worshiping me like a god. I got up off the throne, then walked to what seemed like a balcony. From there, I could see all of Egypt and all the white people in chains working hard under the sun with their black master supervising them. At this moment, I realized I was a pharaoh, so I decided to go outside and walk around, but all my servants argued with me not to go. They said it was dangerous. When I convinced them to come outside with me, they were walking the 3 white men with collars attached to chains like dogs. After I took my third step outside, it began to rain. Then I held my hand out to feel the rain. The water drops turned to drops of wine in my hand. At the sight of this, everyone around me got on their knees and praised me. Then something all white came out of the sky (I believe it was an angel). It approached me and said, "No matter what you do, you cannot escape fate," and gave me a sword made out of diamonds, then disappeared. After that, a war broke out between the white slaves and the blacks. I suddenly appeared in the middle of the battlefield where I saw white people being slaughtered like swine with no weapons. I swung my sword at a man and everything froze.

While everything was frozen in time, I was the only one able to move. So, I swung the sword again and it made a rip in space and time - like it was an entrance to another dimension. I walked up to it and entered the portal. When I entered, the rip was still open but on this side of the portal, the blacks were being persecuted and killed. This dimension was the exact opposite of where I just was. Then I looked at the floor, I saw my body on the floor, headless, with blood everywhere. I have this huge sword that's able to make portals into different dimensions. I was still confused about my purpose in the world I was in, so I made another portal, which took me to the present, where I saw a TV screen with the President and other world officials planning the genocide of Africans. They all had white suits on with big smiles on their faces. Then they looked back at me and said, "We were waiting on you. You were the pharaoh when 3 million white people were killed, so we are going to strike back and kill all you black people before you enslave us again." I didn't know what to say and it was creepy how the TV was watching me and not the other way around. I just made another portal and landed at the school parking lot, where the same angel visited me again and took the sword and said I don't need the sword because my voice was the only weapon I needed. Right at that moment, I saw the cops and they just rode by. Then the school bell rand and everyone formed a crowd around me and stared at me. When I tried to run away, they knocked me down and beat me senseless. Then the police drove by again and arrested me for fighting back. They cuff me, and while I'm being handcuffed, someone recorded what happened on their phone.

Next thing I know, I'm on the news being beaten by the cops while handcuffed. Then a storm of people and cameras waited outside of the jail. When I made bond, the citizens were protesting that I shouldn't have made bond because I was dangerous. They shouted and hollered, "Make America great again!" While I was in my sister's husband's car, they rushed it, banging on the windows and shouting all types of racial slurs. Then my sister's husband turned around looked me in the eyes, and said, "You are nothing but trouble."

When we got home, there was a crowd of angry people out there with signs that the KKK and neo-Nazis use. I got out of the car and ran up to the crowd and suddenly the diamond sword appeared in my hand and I opened a portal, and the other side was black people protesting. At that moment, I realized that the angel didn't want me to fight with my hands but through my words and actions.

After I was done explaining the dream, Keylina said, "Pharaoh, who was your queen?" and after she said that, I had a vivid imagination.

Quan and Kerry both said I needed to stop binge-watching TV at night before I go to sleep. I think they may think I'm crazy or something. The bell rang and it was time to go, so I chugged my milk down and made my way after I threw my lunch tray away.

We all went separate ways to class. I find it ironic how the kid who was bullying me died and I dreamt I drove a car at high speed. It almost makes me feel like I killed him. That's silly for me to feel like that but I do. I'm going to call Carmena when I get home. Maybe she will have something wise to say.

The bell rang, the class was over, and I shot straight home. I passed by the skate park and I saw the goth kids shooting up dope in the snow. Back home, there are crack heads and stuff but I have never seen someone put a needle in their arm. That was a first for me.

I made it home safe, but I keep on seeing those kids shoot the dope up every time I blink. Life is confusing, man. Why do people do drugs that could kill them? I don't understand. The good die young and everyone mourns the death of the bad guy. In a way, I guess life needs the good and the bad because one can't be without the other. Love wouldn't exist without hate but God existed without the devil. This type of thinking is stressing me out. I'm going to take a nap and call Carmena when I wake up.

When I woke up, I walked into the kitchen and got some food, since I hadn't eaten all day. While I was in the kitchen, my nephews were watching TV in the living room. Then my sister's husband walked in drunk as shit. He walked up to me and just size me up like how the boxers do before a fight. This guy is all in my grill. I could smell the alcohol on his breath. I tried to walk around him but he grabbed me by the shirt and told me that I better stay out of his way or he would fuck me up. Then he let me go and pushed me out the way. So I just made my way to the room.

While I was in there, he yelled out loud," I work my ass off to feed my children, not this freeloading, good for nothing ass nigga." After he said that, he threw my food away. I hate this man. I don't know what I did to him for him to treat me like a dog. If my sister was here, grumpy man wouldn't have said or done none of that shit. Jamesha would have put him in his place. He knows what he's doing. My sister works two jobs. If anything, she is the one that pays the bills and puts food on the table, not your bum ass. What type of man lets his woman work two jobs while you stay home and watch TV? This stuff has gone out of hand, man, I can't wait to go home and get out of here.

I lay down on the bed and called Carmena but she didn't answer, so I called her again, still no answer. Then I texted her, "Hey, Carmena. How are you doing, beautiful? I was calling to see how you are and stuff. Hit me back when you can."

Since I slept all day, I can't go to sleep now. I think it will be best if I take 2 sleeping pills and watch TV until I get drowsy. While I was up watching TV, Jamesha walked in through the door.

She puts her bag down and joined me on the couch. She goes, "Hey bro, what are you doing up so late?" Then kisses me on the cheek.

I told her I slept all day and that I couldn't sleep but I took sleeping pills. I'm just waiting for them to kick in.

She got up, went into her room, changed, and came back out. Now we just kicking it like the old days. I wanted to tell her how grumpy man was treating me but I didn't want to start a conflict in the house. Jamesha asked me how I was doing in school. I told her the truth. "I'm doing well but since I'm the only black kid in school, people look at me funny and stuff." Then she told me my nephews would get the same treatment from certain kids at school. That didn't surprise me but it baffled me to know that small children are having the same problem as me. I wonder if they were being bullied but didn't tell anyone. The thought of it made me furious. That was when I told my sister that I loved her and I wouldn't trade her for anybody else. I also told her that I respect her for working hard to make sure that we are fed and have a roof over our heads. After that, I broke down in tears because I was overwhelmed with emotions and I never had an actual moment to articulate myself until now.

Jamesha hugged me tight and held me in her arms until I finally fell asleep. To me, moments like that is what love is all about; being able to provide comfort for those you love and being able to receive comfort and being able to confide in someone that you know won't hurt you. My sister and I were never that close but that moment made my heart bigger, like when the Grinch realized what Christmas was close. Our bond got tighter, like the windpipe of a person that has asthma when they're running.

When I woke up, to my surprise, my sister was there, sleeping in an uncomfortable position. She looked so peaceful. My sister is a queen in my eyes and in that moment, I decided I will spoil her later on in life for all the sacrifices she has done for me. I woke her up, told her to go in her room but she opened her bloodshot red eyes, dozed off, and took the space I was sleeping in, and kicked her legs up.

By now, it was time for me to get prepared for school. When I checked my phone, it was 5:53. I had an hour before it was time for me to start walking. It only took me 10 minutes to get to school and class begins at 7:30 anyways. Today is Friday and that means I don't have to wake up early tomorrow, even though I am going to anyways.

Watching cartoons with my nephews is a great way for me to start my day. Those kids are always so full of life and energy. If something were to happen to my nephews, all hell would break loose. I won't spare no one! My phone died when it was lunchtime. I had to put my phone on silent but it kept on vibrating in my pocket. I know my notifications were from various social media websites but I haven't had the time to check it.

I'm sitting with Keylina and Kerry. I guess Quan didn't come to school today. Keylina is fine as hell for real today. She's wearing black tights and her slim body is speaking to me. While I'm doing my usual glare at her, she asks me if I have seen the video of that girl being gang banged at a college party in front of everyone. I told her no, my phone was dead, and I don't even like watching porn.

At that moment, I found it as a perfect opportunity to tell Keylina the way I feel about women that do those type of things. Keylina motioned to me to show me the video on her phone but I declined. Then I said I can't stand women that don't respect themselves. How could a woman let a group of 3 or more guys go inside her while there's a crowd of people spectating? To me, that doesn't make sense and the worst part is, they have the whole ordeal on video for the whole world to see. If my daughter ever takes part in something like that, I would disown her and tell her she brought shame upon my family. I also said that I don't respect men that take advantage of women that are under the influence of drugs. Personally, I wouldn't get down like that.

Then I fucked up when I told Kerry and Keylina I was a virgin. They looked at each other and laughed so hard their faces turned red. That was when I started sweating and stuff got awkward. After they were finished laughing, Keylina said that it was cute that I was still a virgin. She also said that I look like the type of guy that has had a lot of sex. I was flattered but it was still a weird vibe in their midst. My ears felt like they were on fire. That's how unpleasant this convo got.

Then I asked if they were virgins, and they both said yes. When I thought about it, that was very typical of them to say that but then again, I could go for it. They don't seem like they have had sex. All the females that had sex at redneck high were cigarette smoking, binge drinking whores. Keylina and Kerry don't look like those types. Keylina looks like she has too much self-respect to let someone get inside her without marrying her first. Kerry looks like boys are the last thing on her mind and I know she wants to be with a brother, and the only other brother beside me is Quan, and he is an Oreo; black on the outs, but white on the inside.

The bell rang and the exit to this convo was open, so I told them I would see them around and bounced with the sweat under my armpits feeling like the mud that moves under your boot.

School went by swiftly today. Yeah, teachers and students were still talking about that Chase kid but he is long gone from my memory now. I only remember him when I hear people bring him up. Today went by so well because it is Friday and all the students were planning to get drunk at Steve Wentz's house. I guess every year he throws this big boxing match party in his garage. All it really is, is a whole bunch of teens drinking while watching two drunk guys beat the crap out of each other. You know, basic redneck stuff. Man, the stuff people do here is unexplainable. Since there is nothing to do most of the time, everyone gets drunk most of the time. North Dakota is the state with the most drunk driving accidents in the U.S. but has the smallest population. This place is all messed up. One time, I saw a guy walk his dog while he drove his ATV four-wheeler in the snow. The weirdest shit happens in the middle of nowhere.

The only good thing is that the oil boom over here causes every job to pay very well. That is the only thing this place has on Florida. Back home, jobs are hard to find and they don't pay well. People are out there breaking their back for 8 dollars an hour. That's why the crime rate is high; most guys don't want to work for the white man for peanuts while the white man is eating steak. Think about it. A bag of weed is 10 dollars. If you sell 10 bags, you make 100 dollars and you could sell 10 bags in an hour, so that means you made 100 dollars in an hour while someone is slaving for 8 dollars. That's the problem, the minimum wage needs to be raised in Florida.

Life is hard down south. Most people are on food stamps and are living on paycheck to paycheck. Meanwhile, the children in North Dakota never even heard of the struggle. Most of the kids at my school have their own car. Their parents bought it for them or they paid for it with the money they got from their part- time job. I have also been thinking about getting a job. I mean why not, I have nothing better to do. Most of the time, I'm at home playing video games or scrolling through the timeline of a blog online. The only problem is I may need Grumpy to take me to work and back. That may cause a problem because that dirtbag is always in his feelings. He wears his emotions like a shirt. It never fails. Every day is something with him. He acts just like a little girl, always complaining. I should be the one upset because I was the one fooled into coming here. It's not like I would have come had I known I would be stranded until I graduate. I would have never packed my clothes and just stayed home.

The worst part is Grumpy treats me like he never lived at my mom's house for about 3 years. Who does that? Like you didn't pay any bills for 3 years and call me a freeloader when you finally got a place. What a real piece of shit you are, Grumpy.

I got home and everything was normal. The kids were watching TV. Grumpy was in his room and my sister was at work. I took my shoes off and gave my nephews hugs, then opened the fridge. I grabbed a plastic cup with fruit punch in it and drank it, then closed the fridge and threw the cup in the sink. The fruit punch was much needed. It was so refreshing. Although I was walking in the snow, I was quite thirsty.

On my way to my room, I touched my pocket. Then it came to my attention that I hadn't used my phone all day because it was dead. So, I put my phone on charge once I got into my room, then laid down for a quick second. Then my nephews come racing into my room, laughing and playing. You know how the kids do. Then they ran right back out. I opened my eyes, only to see their backs as they ran out of the room, playing like two puppies.

I got up to close the door behind them. Afterward, I returned to my position laying on the bed until I ended up falling asleep. When I woke up, 3 hours had passed and I looked towards my phone, which had a full charge, 100 percent. I unplugged it from the charger and turned it on. Then, as it was turning on, it started vibrating so much that it made the screen freeze for about 1 minute. The lock screen showed up and I put in my password, then boom, I see all the notifications from my social media accounts.

The first thing I saw was about 30 something notifications, so I clicked on it. After I clicked on it, I saw people tagging me in a video. The video seems to be about a party but the views are in the millions. Right at that moment, once the video began, my heart collapsed and suddenly, life wasn't worth living. Every time I took a breath, it was like I was trying to breathe after running in the snow. My sides were hurting and my head was spinning. I couldn't believe what I was seeing. Impossible, I thought but it was so true. Carmena was on video, being gang banged at a college party. Seeing her being violated like that brought tears to my eyes. We were supposed to get married and take each other's virginity. I watched the video two times and then I was done with it.

Everyone in Miami had seen the video and now Carmena is the laughing stock of the whole city. Millions of people saw this video. I wonder how she feels right now. If she's feeling the way I do, then she feels like an orphan that didn't get chosen to be adopted after being at the orphanage for six years. Carmena, the woman who was flawless to me, suddenly became this disgusting, classless female that didn't deserve my love. Oftentimes, Carmena and I talked about how we hate females that do stuff like that, then she goes on to do the same thing. What a hypocrite she is. I'm so hurt right now, nothing seems to be real. How could this happen to me? My lady is on video, having sex with 5 different guys at a party on a table filled with red plastic cups. The only thing I could think of is, she got drugged and that was actually rape. Carmena is too sophisticated to let this happen, and she would not do something like this. She had to be on drugs. That's all I could think of. Now I'm beginning to question whether she was a virgin or not. A virgin couldn't possibly do something like this.

Why me, God? Why me? Why must I always suffer? I don't understand why something is always happening to me that just ain't right. Like I don't have enough stuff to deal with over here. Now I don't even want to go back home. Carmena was who I was looking forward to when I get home. I can't be with her after this, I would be a fool. My ears are red and hot because I feel so embarrassed. The video is so viral to the extent that people in North Dakota are watching it. I can't marry a woman that will always be remembered as the girl that got fucked on camera at a party by 5 guys. I refuse to accept this fate. This can't be life. Maybe that girl is a look-alike or something. Maybe she has a twin I don't know about.

I would call her to confirm the truth but I can't find the strength to dial her number. This situation would make a horrible conversation. The woman I've been loving for the past 9 years got a train ran on her. What a shame. Life is so unpredictable. You never know what life will throw at you.

I think I'm just going to delete all my social media accounts so I don't have to see this bullshit anymore. Fuck man, why me? I just want to die. Surely this is all a joke or something.

When I wake up, I'm going to laugh at this absurd dream. Carmena would never do that. Damn, I mean she's on the table wasted, eyes closed, being taken advantage of. Some of the comments suggested she had been raped. I'm not sure. How could you sleep while 5 guys go in and out of you in the middle of a party with over 300 people? This doesn't add up. If she was raped, then I could sympathize but I'm still hurt at the fact that the first time I saw Carmena naked was on camera. The worst part is, millions of people saw her like this.

I'm so ashamed right now. I feel like Hillary Clinton when she lost the election. I'm going to stay in bed all weekend. I can't take it. This is too much. The pain I'm feeling is unlike anything I've ever known. I see why the guys back home treat women like shit so they won't have them feeling like I do. I feel like something is missing from my body and my heart is beating to a sad song. Now I know why artists speak the way they do about love. The feeling is mutual. I must be a fool to actually think that my first girlfriend and I were going to get married. How foolish I was to think she would be faithful while I'm over 3,000 miles away. SMH. Love is overrated!

Chapter 3

3 shots of Fireball and 1 cigar was all it took. I was completely wasted. You would think watching some drunk rednecks whoop each other's ass wasn't the best idea. Turns out it's a whole lot of fun. I'm at home staring at the walls and thinking to myself, fuck that shit, let me see what the hype is about. Alcohol and pretty chicks; this seems like the life to live. When I first arrived at the scene, I have to admit everyone was totally shocked to see me pull up. I walked in Steve Wentz's back yard and entered the garage, suddenly all eyes were on me. Luckily I brought a big bottle of Fireball with me, which I purchased thanks to my Uber driver. The only black kid in the whole city was at the party. Normally I wouldn't indulge in this type of behavior, but you only live once. Who gives a shit anyways?

I came in right before the fight started, opened the bottle, and poured myself a shit. Right at that moment, everyone stopped staring at me and I became normal, perhaps even white. I was drinking Fireball in a room filled with teens smoking pot. The smell was so strong I got high off the second-hand smoking. I passed the bottle around because I really didn't buy the shit for myself; it was for the "party".

This extremely gorgeous chick walked up to me and asked me for a shot. I just shrugged my shoulders, trying to be cool. Then she asked for my cup and poured us both shots. At that moment, I started feeling the vibe, she was coming on to me. I'm probably the most goofy person on the earth. I'm totally lost for words, so I just asked her what's her name, and the beauty replied, "My name is Laurie James and I know who you are. You're Jamari." The girl was so drunk she said everything with a slur.

Next thing you know, here comes Steve Wentz. "Aye Jamari, I didn't expect to see you here. Had I known, I would have picked a different playlist for tonight."

I thought to myself that this guy was actually nicer than I thought. Truth be told, I expected him to be an asshole.

He turned to me and said, "Jamari, you got a lighter?" and I said, Neh, bro." Then he looked at me and asked me to step outside with him. At this moment, I didn't know what's coming next. Maybe he's acting cool in front of the crowd and really didn't want me there. As soon as I stepped outside, he pulled out a blunt and lights it up, then he said to me, "Jamari, I'm really glad you came. Here man, hit the blunt."

I looked at him wanting to decline but I was subdued by the peer pressure. My hand began to sweat before he did the handoff. Out of all the times I was pressured to do drugs in the hood in Miami, no one succeeded but here I am today, about to engage in the type of activity I deemed to be foolish. Change happens every five seconds, a wise man once said.

I inhaled one time and instantly my chest felt like a traffic jam. I started coughing and gasping for air. When I looked up after I finished grabbing my knees, Steve started laughing like a hyena. I was embarrassed but the weed took its effect rapidly. All of a sudden I felt like I was floating. That's when Laurie came outside and asked to hit the blunt. I passed it to her with no problem. Crazy how I almost fucking died smoking the blunt and this little white girl is pulling the smoke with no problem. She made me feel like a pussy.

Then all of a sudden, this guy comes out and says someone wants to fight me. My heart started beating fast and I was about to actually box this guy but I thought about it. That's what they want, for the black guy to agree to this foolery. I declined by saying I don't want to blow my high.

Then Laurie said, "Yeah man, now go fuck off." It seemed like all she wanted to do was laugh. I was charmed by how nonchalant Laurie was and I started to become aroused by her.

After the blunt went out, we all went into the garage to watch the fight. It was these two guys that graduated last year boxing. When you think about it, watching two people fight is very entertaining, especially if you were fucked up like I was. Humans play fight, which is just as primal as two lion cubs biting and fighting all day. That goes to show, the human race is so similar to animals in so many ways. The urge to reproduce and be the most dominant being are all primal ways of thinking. Well, at least that's how I feel but I can tell you one thing; a lion can't be fucked up like me right now... LMAO!

I can work hard and enjoy myself every now and then. There ain't nothing wrong with that. I'm just buzzing over this girl Laurie. She has been standing next to me since the moment I got here. I think I should make a move or something. The only thing is, what if she isn't feeling that and I push up on her, and then next thing you know, they are going to hang me by the tree in the skate park. I probably end up being chased out of town by a mob with pitchforks and rifles.

While all these thoughts ran through my mind, Laurie looks up at me and grabs my hand. She looks at me as if it were something urgent, so I whisper in her ear to ask her what's up. By the time I start moving towards her, she just kissed me. The moment our lips touched, it felt unlike anything I have ever experienced before.

Right then everything seemed as if time froze and it was only the two of us on the planet. A nice and wet kiss followed by a hug. Then we dashed out of the garage and headed towards the front of Steve Wentz's home.

I was kind of confused because I thought she was looking to get in my car. I came in a Uber, so that would have killed everything. It turns out we were going to her car. I'm following behind her, she's just leading the way. By now all types of thoughts were running through my mind. The main one was, are we going to have sex? because I'm still a virgin and I would be ashamed of myself if I did a terrible job having sex with her. Plus, I don't think my cock is big enough to please her.

I'm excited but afraid of what awaits me shortly. 30 seconds later, I'm staring at a Dodge Ram pickup truck. The usual in North Dakota. These people here love trucks.

Laurie grabs her keys, unlocks the doors and I stand outside waiting patiently in the snow, for what I don't fucking know. She enters through the driver's side and opens the passenger side and says, "Get in dummy!" I entered the car cautiously, hoping not to leave the wrong impression. Then Laurie looked at me and started the car and turned on the heater because the car was ice cold. Then she pulled away and drove off, so I said, "Where are we going?"

Laurie replies, "You ever been to that trail by the train tracks where everyone goes to ride their dirt bikes and stuff?"

I said, "Nah, I'm new around here."

She smiled and just said, "You'll see pretty soon."

By the time we got there, I was halfway sleepy. The car ride had been really quiet. I was really watching her smoke her cigarette while listening to country music. All I could really say was, the silence wasn't awkward, it was magical. Things seem as if I knew Laurie all my life. She was just real like that. Her smile was insanely gorgeous and she had pretty long black hair. Laurie was about 5'8 which was the perfect size for me. Small, petite physique, but her personality was full of life. Always smiling, joking, and laughing. I know she was always the life of the party wherever she went. I'm just staring at her, lost in her beauty when she stops the car and says, "We're here!" I look to my left and my right and I can't see shit. All I know is we are about 20 minutes away from any main road. I glance at Laurie and she says, "Jamari, where are you from?"

"Miami, Florida," I respond.

"You sure a long way from home, ain'tcha?"

I smile, "Yeah, but it's alright over here. It ain't no violence or any gang shooting or any of the madness that goes on back home. Over here, it's real alright. What about you?"

"I'm a North Dakota native. I would love to go to Miami one day."

Chapter 4

Laurie and I made a wildfire in the middle of a snowstorm. Last night was marvelous. It felt real; almost too real. Never in my life did I imagine myself being in the middle of snow-covered mountains enjoying passionate, steaming hot sex. Well, at least I think that's what happened last night. All I could remember was my lips touching hers and the rest was a blur from there. I'm just now waking up and I feel like there is a fire burning in my body. I also feel so nonchalant.

The car is still running. There are snowflakes on the windshield, and Laurie is still asleep like the angel she is. Staring at her is like looking at jewelry. The only thing is, there is no glass case. While I'm staring at Laurie romantically, all I could see from the corner of my eyes is 2 deer walking without any worries in the world. To me, that was some sort of a sign that maybe I and Laurie were meant to be together. The forces of the universe brought us together for a reason. So many questions running through my head at this point. Was I meant to marry a white woman? What about Carmena? What am I supposed to do? Did I really lose my virginity? Is this how things are supposed to be?

All of a sudden, I started feeling confused. I felt like I was doing the wrong thing. Then I took one more glance at Laurie and knew that love was the most important thing in the world. It was as if, with all the flaws Laurie has, she still seemed flawless. I wished that moment could last forever. Right then and there, I knew I wanted to get married. There is so much beauty in a woman while she sleeps, it's the most gorgeous thing in the world.

The snow, the deer, Laurie. I actually might start to enjoy being in North Dakota. My phone has been off all night since I got to the party and I'm not going to turn it on. The only thing I will have is a thousand calls from my sister, telling me to come home. The funny thing is, this experience makes me want to call North Dakota home. I don't have anything going for me in Miami anyways. Carmena was the only thing that made me want to go back. Now, it's like I don't even want to see her face. I'm so ashamed of myself because of her. She damaged my heart and my reputation. If she loved me, she would have never engaged in those types of activities. I really thought we were going to get married. I loved Carmena more than anything; I held her so far above my head. This was really unbelievable to me. The way she carried herself, I would have never expected this from her. What really hurts is the fact that I have to replay the image of her being violated in my mind over and over.

My heart feels so heavy. The weight of itself causes it to collapse. While all of these crazy thoughts are running through my mind, Laurie wakes up.

She looks at me and smiles, then said, "Good morning, Bud." I replied, "Good morning." She took a little while to fully wake up but once she got up, she started the car and we were off. It didn't take us long to arrive at Laurie's house. Her home was huge with burgundy bricks and a chimney. In Miami, they didn't make houses with chimneys. I thought they only existed in movies. After coming here, I now realize that they are real.

I was kind of scared coming to her place because her parents might be racist or they might be tripping because she didn't come home last night. To my surprise, no one was home but her blue nose pitbull. The dog rushed me, started sniffing, and jumping on me in an unorderly fashion way how dogs do. I guess it was her first time smelling a black guy. The pitbull was so fucking big, it was ridiculous. My only thought was, if it snows most of the time, where does the dog pee and shit? I thought about it and realized I don't really give a fuck. I'm inside the home of a beautiful white girl.

While I was thinking about all of this, I realized my breath smelt like 10 cans of back that ass up. Plus, I needed to take a piss.

I asked Laurie where is the restroom once we got to her bedroom, and she said, "Last room on the right." I walked out of the room and started looking around at the walls. The house was big and spacious but it was barely furnished. I'm guessing that they don't have time to buy new furniture. Either that or they don't care. I surely don't. They must have just moved here; there are still boxes in the living room.

When I entered the restroom, it was nice and clean. I lifted the toilet seat and took my John out, then started pissing my life away. I was so relieved, urinating never felt so good. Now the only thing that needed to be fixed was my hot ass breath. Luckily, there was mouthwash on the sink. Right when I was about to grab the bottle, BOOM! "Aye, Jamari. If you want to take a shower, go ahead," Laurie said. My heart dropped all the way into my ass to the point I could have shit it out. Now that Laurie scared the shit out of me, I started to feel uneasy about being in her house. Still, I stripped all my clothes and took a shower. I took a quick shower, still felt kind of rusty putting on the same old clothes but I was better now.

When I got out of the bathroom, Laurie was fully dressed in new clothes. She apparently took a shower in her parent's bathroom. Laurie fed me, too. She gave me leftover pizza and fruit punch. I was fine with that; I was starving. Laurie's phone started ringing and she looked at me and said, "We got to go, NOW!" We ran out of the house with her dog chasing us.

I didn't know why my heart was racing. Being with Laurie was exciting. I guess it's just the feeling of not knowing what's going to happen next. With her, I'm always on my toes. Sad to say, I'm in love with this girl and it's only been about 12 hours. Here I am in the car with her again. This time something was up and I ain't just talking about my self-confidence.

Something is clearly bothering her. I'm guessing it was the phone call she got. The call was probably from her parents. No big deal, I just hope she's not in trouble.

During this whole car ride, Laurie and I never really spoke. I was still wondering where we were going. The funny thing is, right when I thought that, she asked me where my house is. I said, "It's on Reclamation Drive, by Kum and Go gas station." "Okay, that's right by the school."

"Yeah, not too far from there."

"Cool, I'll have to stop by one day and finish what we started." "I guess so."

"So Jamari, when am I going to see you again?"

"At school, maybe. Well, do you mean as in going out? Like on a date?" "Yeah silly, I just have to see you again. I really enjoyed spending time with you."

"Me too. I had a lot of fun. You're really cool and you have a vibrant personality."

"Thank you, Jamari. Well, I'm here. Where do we go?"

"Turn right there into that apartment complex." "What's your number, Jamari?"

"I don't even know. Ummm, just give me yours. Shit, my phone is dead. I'll just see you at school."

"Okay. Wait, one more thing."

"What?" Then BAM! Laurie gave me the sweetest kiss of my life. I could honestly say that moment was very bittersweet. I loved that I was kissing her but the reason was what made me sad. At some point, our little getaway had to end but, in the meantime,, it felt like forever.

"Bye."

"Bye." The car door thuds and she drives off after I walk into my building. I started to miss Laurie and that's when I realized I fucked up. I didn't get her number. She most likely thinks I'm the biggest douche bag on earth. Hmm… but I still got the chance to see her at school. Realizing that I messed up a good thing makes me feel weary. I don't think I'm good enough to please a woman and besides that, who would want to be with me? I'm a loser.

When I got to my apartment door, that's when I remembered; I didn't come home last night. My sister is going to freak out. A young black man in a town dominated by white people. I know she is worried sick right now, especially because she doesn't have anywhere to go look for me.

Chapter 5

At that moment, I was just pacing back and forth in front of the door, reluctant to enter, afraid of the unavoidable consequences. I might as well go in and get this over with. When I finally gathered the courage to enter the house, I turn the door handle and it's locked. Then I hear from behind the door, "Who is it?"

Now my heart starts to beat like a marching band. Then, after the sounds of the door unlocking, the door swings open. With no surprise, it was my sister. "Jamari, where have you been? Are you okay? Come in, come in. Are you hungry?" My sister is bothering me with all these questions. I don't understand why she is being so nice.

"No, I'm not hungry. I just want to go to bed."

"Okay, lil' bro." Then my sister gives me a nice and tight hug. "I love you, Jamari. I would have been hurt if something had happened to you. Please, Jamari, stay out of trouble. This is no place for a young black man. Police is killing folks out here and Donald Trump got all the rednecks hyped up. Promise you will stay out of trouble."

"I will, sis, and I love you too." That was certainly not what I was expecting. My sister started crying as I was on my way to my room. I thought I was going to get the business.

My nephews, Javon and Marvin, were right in front of the TV. They were so caught up, they didn't even look back to see who came in the house. I'll speak to those badass kids another time. Now is the time for me to jump in my bed and relax. I feel kind of bad though, my sister is crying because I didn't come home. I have to make more rational decisions; my actions don't only affect me. They also affect those around me.

Laying on my bed, reflecting on the crazy night I had with Laurie, just thinking about it brings joy to my face. I had to laugh at myself. Man, I was so drunk that I don't even know if we had sex or not. If we did, you would think I would remember.

My sister was worried almost to death about me. The words that stuck the most with me was, "This is not a place for a young black man." Only to think, in modern-day America, one year after we had a black President reign for 8 years and there are still certain areas where a black man cannot be. Several years after the civil rights movement, here I am still finding out that I was born with a disability... my black skin. It really is a shame to know this is still a problem when all people belong to the human race.

Tossing and turning, going in, and going out of sleep. Thinking about Laurie, Carmena, and the stress of being a black man. Society doesn't want to see me become successful. The one I loved the most broke my heart, the only love I ever knew was destroyed. The remains of my heart were sent to the land of the null and void, only to be recovered in a land that was never discovered. It's like when it all comes down to it at the end of the day. No matter how much fun you can have with another person, the one you love is what really matters to you. At this point, I'm starting to feel guilty for cheating on Carmena, even though she engaged in such a dishonorable act. Honestly, I feel like I shouldn't feel bad because of what she did. I also feel so dull. I really don't know how to feel. There are so many emotions I'm currently experiencing, I can't even really describe the way I feel. All in all, I would have to say my heart and my mind are at war and my emotions are the battlefield.

By the time I got into a deep sleep, I had already recalled everything that had happened to me in the past weeks. I went to sleep knowing that I would wake up a changed man. Something had to change. I did drugs for the first time and I liked it. Plenty of people smoke weed and drink alcohol. That doesn't mean they are junkies. It's crazy how one night can have such a big impact on your life. I'm just happy my sister didn't notice I got fucked up last night.

I don't know if it was the marijuana or the liquor but I had the most peculiar dream. I was walking down a real dirty street and a poverty-stricken neighborhood in Port Au Prince, Haiti. Smoke was in the air and there was such a foul smell lingering. As I was walking around, I was looking at the homes made out of strips of metal. There was a woman selling food on the street out of a metal grill. They used some sort of cheap charcoal, which made the smoky smell in the streets. On another side of the streets, there was a group of guys playing dominoes and one guy was standing up, wearing a pink dress. A lot of the guys were extremely loud and drunk. Everything was so foggy. It was a sight I had never seen before but it felt like I was always around this type of stuff. There were guys selling drinks on the corner out of a water cooler.

The entire time I was walking down this road, I never knew where I was going, I was just walking. It was as if I were a ghost. I was capable of seeing everyone but nobody seemed to notice me.

That all changed when my eyes stumbled on a black cat with emerald green eyes. I looked at the cat and it started running, then it stopped and turned around. At first, it seemed like a normal black cat but when I saw those ominous green eyes, I knew something was up. I started to get scared. My body temperature started rising. I planned to run away but my legs kept on moving towards the animal. With every step I took, the faster my heartbeat was. Before I knew it, I was 10 steps away from the strange feline. Those green eyes locked onto me and the cat moved towards me. By this point, I'm in complete fear, looking down on a four-legged animal, feeling

46

helpless. The cat looked up at me and said, "It's an illusion. Everything you think you know is an illusion, nothing is real. Everything is fake, it's all an illusion."

I was so shocked that I couldn't even respond. A cat was speaking to me as if it were some divine being. I was trying to run and scream but I was unable to. "Do you want to be seated with the gods or do you want to sit with the mortals? Life and death is all an illusion. The soul never dies, it's an illusion." The next thing I heard was "Boom, Boom" the sounds of someone beating a drum. Suddenly, I was in the middle of a voodoo festival. There were at least 500 people. The first thing that stuck to me, other than the drums and the chanting coming from a man with a green hat was a man on the floor, shaking violently. This was chaos to me but there were also beautiful women in tribal clothes with paint on their faces, dancing. Little kids were running around. They seemed to be eating something but I can't tell exactly what it was.

I was curiously looking around but I was still in terror. Then all eyes shifted on me and the man in the green hat looked at me and said something Creole I couldn't understand but at the same time, I understood. It was as if we spoke telepathically.

Everything was so strange how I ended up in the middle of a voodoo ceremony. Two women brought the priest two chickens and he chopped their heads off with a small but sharp blade. All you could see from there was blood in the air and the two headless chickens, running. I seemed to be the only person worried. Everyone looked happy to me. Some people were smoking, drinking, playing an instrument, or dancing. The craziest thing I ever imagined. I wanted to know why everyone was looking at me. It was because the chicken blood never hit the floor. The blood stayed in the air, just levitating, defying all of the laws of physics as we know it.

The priest looked at me and poured the blood on me, then the crowd rushed me. I was bathed by everyone. Some guys poured their drinks on me, some people rubbed leaves. It was so uncomfortable. The blood and everything that touched my body stung. I tried to move but I was paralyzed. I was left in the hands of those savages.

Chapter 6

The priest with the green hat touched my head and pulled out his knife. He sized me up, then Boom!!! I wake up with my heart pounding in my chest and sweat all over my body. I was scared for my life.

Then I heard my sister yell "Jamari!!!" at the top of her lungs. She sounded worried. It was the type of yell you would hear when a person falls down a cliff because you lost your grip and couldn't save them. My heart dropped when I heard her. She started banging on my door. I got up, hesitant to open the door but eager to see what was the commotion all about. When I turned the knob, all I could see was my sister's eyes, flaming red, with tears coming down her face.

I asked her, "What's going on?" "Are you okay?"

"Yeah, I'm fine. What's up with you?"

"Nothing. I heard you yelling and shouting. I thought something was wrong with you."

"I was sleeping. Was I really shouting in my sleep?" "Yes, you were, and you were speaking Creole."

"Are you serious?"

"I'm just glad to know that you're fine. I love you, bro. If you need me, I'll be here."

I don't know what's going on but I don't like it. Why was she crying because I was yelling and my door was locked? While all of these thoughts were processing in my mind, I got a sudden feeling of despair. It was as if I got shot in my stomach. The pain was unbearable. Something had to be going on but I just didn't know what. That's when I decided I should call Carmena, so I can remove this guilt off my chest. The guilt was killing me, knowing I betrayed my lover like that made me ashamed of myself. How could I be the same type of person I despise? I got high, drunk, and I cheated on my girl. I always thought I was bigger than that and I couldn't be just like the guys from my hood. Turns out that I'm no better than any of those guys. Different minds and ideals still have the same primitive need to please themselves, not caring about those affected by the actions they do.

Maybe it's not guilt that's killing me. Yeah, I may be a piece of shit for getting high and cheating but that's not the core of my problems. I'm liking the lifestyle I lived last night. The feeling I have might be my old self dying within me. That just might be the formation of the man I am supposed to become.

I'm going to call Carmena and explain to her that I'm a changed man now. I don't know what's going on with me right now. I'm still having problems with the dream I just had and my sister is crying because she's worried about me. Why am I even caring about Carmena? She doesn't love me. It's been about 2 days since I heard from her anyways. If she cared, she would have called me or something. You know what? Maybe I'm thinking a little too irrational. I should put myself in her shoes. She didn't call because she is embarrassed. I need to call her and let her know, no matter what, I'll be there for her. It must be tough, going through all that scrutiny. Everything isn't all about me. There are always two sides to a story. I want to know what she has to say about this. Carmena knows better than that. Someone had to drug her or something. She's too intelligent to let this happen.

I'm getting depressed just thinking about the dreadful video. The image of her being degraded haunts me. Millions of views, people all over the globe are still viewing this. I'm going to get this over with already and call her.

Shit, my phone is dead. I didn't plug it to charge. I'll put it on charge now and get something to eat. I will call her when I get back from the kitchen. I'm hungry, man. What I ate at Laurie's was nothing.

On my way to the kitchen, I see my nephews sitting in front of the TV.

I decided to see what the youngsters been up to. "Hey, Jovan and Marvin, what are y'all up to?"

"Nothing, uncle. We're just watching TV" "Y'all have been watching TV all day."

"It's snowing outside and we can't play in the snow. Mom doesn't want us to get sick and we were about to play video games, uncle."

"Okay, I love you guys." "Yeah, we know."

"So, you're not going to say I love you back."

I spoke with them, then I walked away, amazed by the small talk I had with my nephews. Those two boys are just adorable, man. They sometimes act like they don't want to talk to me because of their little kid's shy ways. I use to be the same when I used to speak to adults. The only thing is, I'm not an adult, so they shouldn't feel that way.

When I got into the kitchen, I opened the fridge and there was juice, leftovers, fruits, and some other snacks. I didn't have any interest in those items, so I closed the fridge door and went to the pantry. There was cereal but we had no milk, so I just grabbed a bag of potato chips from a variety pack of chips. Even though I had already found my snack to quench my hunger for the moment, I went looking through all of the shelves in the kitchen. To my surprise, I found nothing. I continued to search the kitchen until I realized it was pointless. I already found something to eat, so I went to my room after a drink of water.

When I entered my room, it still had this gloomy feeling to it. I can't really exactly describe how it felt, I was just creeped out by being in there.

The room was also hot, steaming hot. The heater is on but the temperature was higher than normal. I cracked open my window slightly, so I could get some cold air in the room, then I reached for my phone on the charger.

I turned on my sleek metallic smartphone and searched through my contacts to call Carmena. I called her once, it made the dial sound but she didn't answer. I kept calling her with no success. I was so upset because she didn't pick up her phone. Which was so unlike her but lately, everyone has been acting different. That's when I decided to send her another text message, "Carmena... I want to talk..." Now I'm just wondering what's going through her mind. How could she not answer? Before I went to the party, I deactivated all of my social media accounts because the backlash from my internet peers was too much. All of the notifications were too mean for me to handle and that video was too painful for me to watch. That was the only thing on my timeline. Maybe the site died down by now.

I put my email address in and my account looked as if I never deactivated it. I have the same profile picture and the same amount of followers. I took one scroll down the page and saw the most shocking thing in the world. I dropped my phone in complete disbelief. "No! No! No! No! No! That's not fair!" It was Carmena's old best friend, Paris Jenkins. She posted something saying "R.I.P. Carmena, you were too young #cyberbullyingmuststop".

Beep!

All I could hear was a buzzing sound in my ear. The room was soundless, it was so silent you could hear an ant crawl. Why me? I thought to myself. It seems like my life was meant to be lived in misery. No matter what I do, nothing is going to change. My only friend is my suffering. How will I ever get the chance to overcome this?

Ding! Ding!

That's when the bell began to ring in my head. There must be another Carmena out there. I have to get to the bottom of this. I'm going to call her one more time.

I said this knowing she wasn't going to answer. I was only lying to myself.

At that moment, I was scared and confused, not knowing what to think, so I turned back to social media. I began to look at my phone curiously and discouragingly. The feeling of not knowing is killing me and keeping me alive. There is no way I could survive the death of the love of my life. If Carmena is actually dead, some other woman will be crowned the most gorgeous woman on the planet. I'm horrified. The thought of losing Carmena is overwhelming. Still, somewhere in the back of my mind, I knew I was giving up hope too fast. I must find a solution. Even though I'm scared of the truth, my heart will never be at rest if I don't confirm the breaking news.

By now, my stomach is feeling very uneasy and my palms are sweating like Lebron James at halftime. My heart is hollow like a cave and it feels heavier than an 18 wheeler.

This is absurd. I can't believe I am actually believing this bullshit. My sister would have told me if Carmena passed away. That's it, I'm going to ask Jamesha what's going on. Boom! That's when I put two and two together. That's why my sister been so worried about me. She must have thought I knew. I jumped up off my bed, threw my phone down, and went to my sister's room.

"Hey, Jamesha. I saw someone post R.I.P. Carmena. Do you think they are talking about our Carmena?"

"Yeah, it's true," my sister said, sniffling. "You lying. What happened?"

"They said she killed herself because of the video. I was told that people were bullying her online and she couldn't take it." I stayed mute, unable to summon the strength to talk. "She overdosed on molly. She took 10 grams and her heart stopped. It is sad. I never would have thought Carmena was on drugs. Be strong and keep your head up. I'm here if you need me, bro."

"Did they do an autopsy?"

"I don't know but the story is all over the news."

Tears running down my face like a stream. Every day I live is like a dream. When is my pain coming to an end? Seems like my tears are my only true friend. Always there when I need it the most.

I said nothing and walked to my room, locked the door. I broke down and started sobbing like a baby. My girlfriend is dead, she overdosed on drugs. I'm only 17, I'm not supposed to be going through this. How can this be? I'm just wondering how she died. Did she overdose on drugs by mistake? Or did she take too much to die deliberately? When did she even start doing drugs? This is all my fault. If I didn't move to North Dakota, she would still be alive because I would have been with her. She would still be here with me right now, laughing with her wonderful smile. God, why do all the good people die young? God please, this isn't true. This can't be real. Lord, why do you hate me? What have I done to you for me to deserve this? I know we don't speak often but I'm not a bad guy. I try my best to do what's right.

Carmena, we were supposed to live the rest of our lives together. How could you leave me like this? The last time we spoke, I told her I love her. That's crazy, ain't it? At least I can say that. It was the dope that led her to do that crazy stuff. That's got to be it. Man, I didn't even get the chance to really speak with her before she passed. Fuck God. God can't be real because if he was, he wouldn't let this happen. Life is a constant assault on the angels; no matter how you hold the camera, the picture is the same on every angle. The demons are constantly being praised for the destruction of humanity. Why God, why do I have to suffer? Was I born to live in the heart of misery?

While I was crying, I started thinking about all of the memories, as painful as they are. Carmena and I enjoyed some really good times. I remember when we first met. Look how far I have come since then. Laughing in the hallways, kissing, and touching each other. She was the most beautiful girl I ever laid eyes on. Pondering in all of the memories makes everything more difficult for me to accept. I can't help but blame myself for the death of my lover. Unsure if I will ever be able to love again. Just when I thought I had everything figured out, I realized none of that matters. It's always something that comes along to destroy me. My heart has been shattered into a billion pieces. There is no point in living when you think about it. You do all of this living, just to die at the end. White or black, you still have to die. No matter how much money you have, you can't take it with you once you die. What's the point of living if you're just going to die? It's foolish to think about the opinions and thoughts of others if, when you pass away, they all are going to forget about you. When you die, nobody remembers you after a while. At most, they think about you when your birthday comes but you'll just be a memory. Who cares about driving the best cars or having the finest clothes or having all the women if you're just going to die? After death, life will be like you never existed.

All of your friends will find new friends, your lover will get a new lover. What's the point?

The only way living can have meaning is if you do great in your lifetime. People like Jesus, MLK, Toussiant L have left a permanent mark in history. Even though they passed away, their name still lives on today. These men still have a great impact on the world today. They will forever be known for their bravery. If you don't leave your mark in history, you will have lived for nothing.

I don't know who my grandfather's father is. You can have children but their children's children won't remember or know who you are. What's the point of having kids if they won't acknowledge you years from now?

Life is truly pointless. We live only to die. What's the purpose of being alive in the first place? I should take my own life to end all of my pain. This is too much for me to take in.

I can't do that because then I will bring the same pain I'm going through upon my loved ones. Questioning life, asking questions no one can answer, feeling like a cancer that's destroying mankind. Feeling sorry for myself for having such a horrible life. Surely no one else my age is going through this. The worst part is, I am all the way over here. I can't go to the viewing or the funeral. Well, I could ask my parents to buy my ticket to go to Miami. This just might be my escape card.

Damn, I was looking forward to going back home to see Carmena but not this way. I have to say my last goodbyes to my wife. Even death can't suppress my love for you.

Damn, and I got school tomorrow. I got perfect attendance. I'm not going to let this blemish my record. I really don't feel like going but I'm going to suck it up and be a man. Attending school is already depressing enough as it is, now I have to add this to my plate. I should just stay at home. I have plenty of things on my mind.

Laying in my bed with a nose filled with snot, so I blow my nose on my shirt and discard it. Now I'm half-naked with the crack in the window making me cold, so I get up and close the window and get back in my bed under the covers.

My heart is utterly destroyed and my mind is handicapped by the negative self-talk I'm having. Crying my soul out under the sheets slowly leads me back to sleep.

That's when I had another odd dream. I was on my way to school, walking as normal when I saw the creepy black cat again. The cat was in an alley when I spotted it and it enticed me to follow it. I started trailing behind the cat and the animal said, "I can smell fear on you. There is no need to be afraid." Then the cat stopped and looked at me with these vibrant eyes. The way the creature gazed at me made me feel like it saw my soul. Then the cat said, "Even though it's an illusion, you have to fight!" Then it ran away and I was faced with the challenge of going to school on time.

I followed the cat so far I didn't know how to get back. By the time I woke up from this dream, it was 5:30. School starts in two hours. Hmm, I should lay down and get some more rest. 20 minutes later, I'm laying down, falling in and out of consciousness. Too tired to get up but I have too much energy to sleep. An hour passes by and I get up and get dressed for school. Honestly, I don't want to go but I'm not going to stay home and drooping in self-pity then watch my life dwindle. I got to fight man, I can't give up on myself like that.

As I was putting my boots on, my sister walks into my room and says "You don't have to go to school if you don't want to."

"I want to go. I ain't got nothing better to do." "Okay, I'll drop you."

"Nah that's fine, I'm going to walk."

"Are you crazy? It's snowing too hard. I'm going to drop you off in 5 minutes."

"Okay." Waiting for my sister to take me to school and that's when it hit me, I might see Laurie today at school. I guess this can't be that bad. Laurie and I might be meant to be after all.

I got into the car with Jamesha and the ride was silent all the way to school. When we got to the school, I opened the door and left with one goodbye kiss on my sister's cheek. When I stepped out of the vehicle, the wind chill hit me and I ran inside the building. Things got warm once I entered school.

Chapter 7

On my way to class, I started to feel funny, my stomach started rumbling. I was hungry and scared of going to class all of a sudden I became unsure of whether I should attend school or not.

Walking through the hallways as I see a few kids pass by me with books in their arms and a bag on their backs, no one was paying attention to me but for some reason, I felt like the limelight was on me. The class I was going to start in 2 minutes and only a couple of people there spoke to me before. I guess that wasn't a problem with me. I wish everyone talked to me and treated me like one of their own but I wasn't. I must deal with the cards I have been dealt. Things weren't that tough anyways, people have survived worse. Imagine this, all of the slaves that were tortured for years still made it, so why can't I? There is no excuse I can come up with that can justify giving up on myself.

I made a right turn on the second floor and there were two doors on the left and one on the right. The last door on the right was my class door, only about 15 feet away. As I was approaching my destination, the hallway started feeling like it got longer and longer. Things were as if I was never going to make it to class. My head started spinning, I felt like a dog chasing his own tail, going after something I know I won't get. My stomach began to rumble even louder. I was feeling really dizzy, very dizzy. Surprisingly, I made it to class on time.

When I walked into the room, everyone was looking at me strangely. I felt like a piece of meat and everyone else was wolves waiting to dine on me. While I was going to my seat, I felt something strike my head. Before I knew, I was being jumped by a couple of guys in my class. I guess I got struck on the head with a book. Whatever it was, it really hurt. When I got hit, I dropped to the floor and felt I was being surrounded by a lot of people. I'm lying on the floor helpless, while I'm being beaten senseless by some hillbillies. Then I lost consciousness... The last few things I saw was boots and blue jeans, and a bottle of soda on the floor next to me. Everything took place so quickly I didn't have time to react.

I woke up wondering, what the fuck? Where am I? I'm looking around and all I can see is blurred lines. I tried to get up but my body was too stiff to move. At the realization of this, I began to panic. I'm uncertain of my location and my body isn't functioning. Then I heard a beeping sound in the distance, ringing at a constant pace. Beep! Beep! Beep!

That's when I noticed I'm in a hospital, lying on one of those beds. I must be paralyzed, I thought to myself. Things can never get better for me, I always end up in some fucked up situation. I can't believe this. I'm paralyzed. Those guys beat me, now I'm unable to move from the neck and below. I might as well die because there ain't nothing I could do besides think to myself.

Now I'm all worked up, scared, and angry at being half-dead. Lying on a hospital bed, wondering what happened to me. Am I going to survive? Am I going to die? The only thing I know for sure is, I'm in critical condition. I'm hooked to a machine. Well, I think I am.

I got tired of all my awful thoughts and took a nap. When I woke up this time, I looked to my left and my right. I was in the room by myself. My arm was hooked up to an IV to shoot drugs into my system. The noise I heard earlier in the day came from the rooms on the other side of the curtain. There were other patients in worse condition than I was. My body felt fine. I'm guessing it was the medication that had me feeling unable to move. The drugs are so strong I could taste it every time I breathe. I feel better now, at least I'm not paralyzed. It's funny when I come to think about it, I always assume the worst in every situation.

One day later, I got transferred from the Intensive Care Unit to regular care patients. When I got to the regular care unit, that's when my family was able to come to see me.

The entire time before my transfer, I was really sad, man. I mean I'm grateful to be alive but my life sucks. Everything is going down the drain. I'm on a thin line between life and death. I want to cross over so I can be with my wife, Carmena but only God knows where her soul is. My life is that old beat-up car that has been through so much but still, it keeps on going.

Jamesha showed up to the hospital with Jovan and Marvin but her husband didn't come. I don't give a fuck anyway. I don't consider him family anyway. I was happy to see my kin. I felt like I haven't seen them in years.

Confined by these hospital walls, being held captive for my own safety. My sister also brought some food. It smelt really good, way better than the bullshit they served in here. She brought a burger and some fries with orange soda. I ate the food like I was unsure if I would get the chance to eat again. The meal was great; it really cheered me up.

The look on my nephew's face was also really funny. They were looking so weird and nervous, until finally, Jovan said, "Hey uncle, what happened? Are you okay?"

"Yeah, I'm fine."

"When you get better, will you play cards with us?"

"Sure, first thing when I get home." Seeing those kids really made my day.

- They are so charming.

When I finished speaking to the kids, I took a glance at my sister and she smiled but at first, she had the worried mother face. So I told her, "Wassup sis? How are you doing?"

"Boy, I'm doing fine, and you?"

"I'm good, man. I can't wait to get out of here, man."

"I want to know what type of medication they are giving you because you sound real sleepy."

"I don't even know, and sis, what happened to the kids that jumped me?"

"You didn't get jumped. What happened was you had a panic attack and fell and hit your head really hard. The doctor said you have anxiety and depression and that you will be taking medication from now on to help you with this."

"Are you serious? A panic attack?"

"Yeah. You are over-stressed out, the doctor recommends you stay home for a week or so."

"Okay."

Wow! I had a panic attack from anxiety and stress. This is puzzling because I could've sworn I felt someone hit me with a book in my head, and I felt the guys kicking me and stuff on the floor. I wanted to try to explain to my sister what happened but that would have created an argument I know I won't win. You can never win an argument with women.

"Oh yeah, the doctor said you should be getting ready to leave in a few hours after he writes the prescription."

That was the only good news I heard lately. Seeing my folks was cool for the first hour. After that, we ran out of stuff to talk about till we were just staring at each other.

The doctor walked into the room with some papers in his hand and gave them to Jamesha. The papers were my prescriptions. I had to take one pill for anxiety and one pill for pain. The doctor looked like he was in his late 20's, he had to be about 28, 29, maybe 30. He had blond hair, brown eyes, and he was about 6 feet tall. The guy was really nice to me and my family. He explained to me the purpose of having healthy thoughts so I could overcome my depression. I also have a minor concussion but the doc said after two or three days, I'll be fine. Doc handed the discharge forms to Jamesha and I was able to leave.

Exiting the medical rehabilitation center felt like I was being released from prison. Finally, I'll be able to see the free world.

Once I walked out of the hospital and my skin sensed the winter wind, I thought to myself, I'm still in prison. Not physically but mentally and emotionally. In today's society, we aren't free to be ourselves as much as the government and the people want you to believe you're free, we really aren't. The government still controls the food we eat, the clothes we wear, and the TV we watch. Everything has regulations. We also don't make our own ideas, thoughts, or philosophy. We go by what "the man" wants us to think. The people are still slaves to money, cars, and clothes. We are slaves in the sense of working for major companies and we only make a small fraction of their money. When you think about it, we still worked for free.

Chapter 8

Nowadays we are slaves to our phones and social media. Freedom is to be found within the soul and nowhere else. Even a man restricted to living in a cell can be free. Trapped is the man afraid to explore new horizons. He is a slave to society and the pattern set by the elite. The men and women cherished the most in the world didn't follow the rules society made for them, they made new rules for society to follow. Normal is prison and weird is freedom. Everyone must embrace themselves and be the person they were born to be, not the person they see on TV or on the web. Beauty comes from being original, one of a kind. Surely, if there are a thousand gray ducks and one white duck, the white duck will be the most attractive because it's different.

I refuse to be another average Joe when I can be myself. No one can be better than me at being myself. I will not stay in the mental prison they want me to be in. I must break out and become the man I am destined to be. There are two routes in life; the highway that allows you to speed by, and the old dirt road with the potholes that require you to slow down. The highway leads you to hell because it's easy and the old dirt road leads you to Heaven because it's the path less taken. Everyone can be a follower but it takes a man of integrity to lead.

In the car, riding, thinking about how I let society fool me into thinking that being black means you won't be successful and that means life will be harder for me. That's all a lie. I am the person that decides whether I will be successful or not. My future is in my hands and no one else. I am a fool. I really thought those guys in my school are out to get me. These people probably don't worry about me, they have their own lives to live. By downplaying these people, I am no better than them. If I discriminate against them, then I am the very same person I despise. I won't leave a blind eye to what's going on but I will give everyone a chance.

I walked in my home with a sort of a positive attitude, which didn't last long. When I saw my phone, I immediately thought of Carmena. My heart cried at the sight of the cellular phone. Reality sucker punched me. My stomach had an avalanche, everything inside me fell. Positivity left me faster than the Holy Spirit in a strip club. I was now weaker than a man roaming the desert with no water. My eyes are a dam soon to be broken with overflowing water. Understanding as a human the only thing I'm owed is death. All the pain you go through, is life worth the few moments of happiness?

As much pain as the phone brought me, I still have to use it. There is nothing for me to do in this house. Oh shit, I got to find out when is Carmena's funeral. I'm going to call her parents and see what's up. Damn, I haven't called them since I was in Miami. That's fucked up, they probably think I ain't shit because I didn't speak to them the same day she passed away. Maybe I shouldn't call but it would be only right if I called.

Man, WTF am I saying? Mrs. Belle loves me, man. I grab the phone, dial the number, and called. After about three rings, she answered the phone.

"Hello," said Mrs. Belle in a sad, broken voice. "Hello, Mrs. belle. This is Jamari. How are you?" "I'm doing fine, baby."

"That's what's up. I was just calling to see how you are doing, and I wanted to know, when is the funeral?"

"The viewing was yesterday and the funeral is Tuesday." "Thank you, Mrs. Belle. I'm so sorry for your loss."

"Carmena was my baby, but the Lord wanted her to be with him," Mrs. belle said that with a cracking voice, trying hard not to cry over the phone.

"I'm coming down to Miami for the funeral. When I get there, I'm going to let you know."

"Okay baby, I love you."

"I love you too, mom." Click, and I hang up the phone.

I really didn't think Carmena's death was true but speaking to her mom confirmed it. The dam broke loose and tears ran down my face like a stream. I was weeping in full throttle, maximum intensity, shaking my head no, no, no, no, in complete disbelief. The love of my life has really gone... She is no more. I don't know how to deal with this. What can I do?

This medication isn't doing shit for me. I still feel sad. Maybe if I smoked some weed I'll feel better or if I get drunk. I felt pretty good when I was high. Meeting Laurie that day was cool, spending time with her might be good for me.

Damn, I got to get to Miami in time for the burial. I really have to go bury my love. I don't have any money to buy a ticket and I doubt my mom has any money. I know Jamesha is short on cash because her good for nothing ass boyfriend doesn't want to work. All he wants to do is get drunk with his broke ass. I don't think I'm going to make the funeral. The cheapest way to get there is by bus and it's a 3-day ride by Greyhound. I would have to get the ticket tonight if I want to make it on time.

Knowing I won't make it crushed me. I can't even go to one of the most important events of my life. I'm good for nothing. I already spoke to Mrs. belle about everything. I make everything so difficult. Fuck, man.

I was sobbing and wishing God would take my life because clearly, I have no purpose on the earth. Even if I did, I'm sure it wasn't a good one. Everything I touch fails. Carmena would have found a way to make it to my funeral. It's a shame I can't do the same for her. What if I never moved up here? What if she never went to that party? What if Heaven and hell is an illusion and there is no life after death. What if I was white? What if blacks made white people slaves? What if I was rich? I could ask a thousand what-if questions but I can't live life on a what-if. I must do, I must accept the things I cannot change. I will make what's unknown to me my reality through hard work and patience. I can't question life all the time because then I will be too afraid to live it. There are just some things I don't need the answer to.

I'm really stressed out, my life isn't going as I planned it to be. Everything has gone downhill. Sitting on my bed, trying to come up with a master plan, while fighting my demons, feeling like I'm going insane with all this stress and pressure. But you know what they say, pressure makes diamonds. I'm going to come out on top of this, no matter how hopeless things may seem. Self-pity is the worst kind. Man, I have to break this now. How can I be successful? Well, first things first, I must finish my last year of high school so I can get into college, although I don't know what I'm going to major in.

That's where I will start. I should go to school for business. Hopefully one day I'll run a major company. That sounds good but I need money now. I'm going to start putting in job applications everywhere. There is too much money out here man for me to be sleeping like this. Back home I don't have as many opportunities. I have to make the most out of this. I mean, the minimum wage is like 10 dollars. I could get a part-time job, work for 8 hours for 4 days a week, and at the end of 2 weeks, I'll walk home with 640 bucks. That ain't bad at all for a part-time job while I'm going to school.

I have to get my life back on track, I'm losing it. Being cooped up in this house isn't going to help at all. Fuck all that rest shit the doctor was talking about, I'm going to school tomorrow. Then again, I should just chill out and plan things before I go do it. There is nothing to plan really, just attend school, and look for a job. The rest will come over time. Plus, I have medication now, so I won't have to worry about falling out.

All of the excessive thinking, worrying, and crying made me exhausted. My eyes got heavy and then I fell asleep like a Panda. I slept well all night and wasn't disturbed by anything. I woke up and got dressed for school with no problem.

Chapter 9

The only thing is, I woke up extra early so my sister won't see me slip out the door. She would have insisted I stay home and get rest. I was charged up and ready to take on the cold, I live in a snow-filled world. I really didn't have any choice, staying home wasn't an option for me.

I started my walk to school, which was only like 20 minutes away on foot. The class starts in about an hour, so I had an extra 30 minutes to kill beforehand. I'm not going to the store. I refuse to ever go in there again. If I had to choose death or shop at the store, I will purchase my own coffin and pray I meet Carmena on the other side.

While walking, I saw the usual stuff; people who let their dog out in the morning snow to piss and shit. I saw this guy smoking a cigarette with his work clothes on. He had one of those green vests crossing guards wear with a hard hat, big boots, and a thermal jacket. The man was about 6'5, 250 pounds, with a red-haired beard. I mean, he was a big dude. I wouldn't give him any shit. He was standing while his pickup truck was running.

I walked a couple more blocks and saw at the main intersection, right before the school, a very dusty pickup truck with dirty snow stuck to the bottom of it. The car has to be 1999 or something from the '90s, it was so beat up. It made this awful screeching noise, it sounded like a pig squealing for dear life. I saw other vehicles lined up at the red light but that car stuck out the most.

There was also a long line at the local breakfast stop. The drive-through window was overused because it's so cold and no one wants to step out and get their food. If you walk in the restaurant, you will eat faster than those in the drive-through. The line had about 7 cars. It was pretty long considering it's not even 7 o'clock yet.

On my right side was the skate park, which is normally dead around this time of the year. When spring comes around, then the park will have some life again. The skate park was home to weirdos and drug addicts and country boys. The best kind of people North Dakota has to offer. Oddly, I saw a few people at the park from afar. When I crossed the street and got closer, I realized I saw some kids from my school; no big deal. I didn't pay them any mind until I heard someone call my name. I ignored it the first two times. I thought I was tripping out. I turned around, sure enough, it was Steve Wentz speed walking up to me from afar.

I was surprised to see him but also kind of happy. Although I barely know him, he felt like a friend. I shook his hand when he got close enough to me. Then he said, "Aye, Jamari? You have a lighter by chance?"

'Nah, bro but I got a dollar if you want to buy from the store across the street."

"Sure, that will be perfect."

"Here you go." I handed him the money.

"Thanks, bro. I got this blunt, when I come back I will let you hit it."
"Okay, sure."

By the time Steve and I got finished talking, 2 of his stoner friends caught up with us. I greeted them but I didn't get their names. They were just a group of hippies trying to get high.

The boys made their way to the store while I stayed at the park, waiting. While I was walking, I didn't really get cold but waiting for those guys to come back changed that. My hands started to freeze after almost 5 minutes of waiting. I was shivering and all. I was so cold that the little wind that touched my skin felt like a blade slicing my skin. So I stuck my arms in my shirt and left my sleeves just hanging in the meantime. I looked up at the street corner and saw the trio on their way over here. They looked so far away and it felt like they took forever to come. In reality, they were only gone for about 10 minutes and they were only 2 minutes away. The 3 guys were headed towards me. When they arrived, I was looking at them in awe. To me, they were some badass dudes that didn't give a fuck about anything. I also kind of have a man-crush on Steve Wentz. He threw a big party at his house, where I met a wonderful girl named Laurie. I smoked weed for the first time with him and I was drunk as hell. I had the time of my life that night, imagine how he is living. His life must be interesting. I think Steve is a cool guy, laid back, and he's not racist at all, not one bit.

The funny thing is, I'm colder than an ice fisherman while these guys don't even feel a thing. They are acclimatized to this weather so it doesn't bother them.

When Steve and his guys came to the gazebo, they started talking shit about the asshole store clerk. He accused them of stealing, which wasn't surprising because he did the same to me. I was kind of happy to hear that because I know that the guy isn't racist, he's just a bigot. Here I am thinking that I'm going through shit just because I'm black and the whites are going through the same shit as me. That goes to show, black or white, we all the same. We all are a part of the same race... the human race.

While Steve and his homies were busy talking about the store clerk, Steve fired up the blunt. A rumble in my stomach initiated. I was unsure if I was making the right move. Smoking pot before school wasn't the best thing to do. Plus, someone lied against me once before, saying they saw me smoking. Now that I'm actually performing the act I was accused of, I might be in deep shit if caught. Fuck that, no one can see us from here anyway, plus I'll just say I'm on my anxiety medication.

Smoking weed that night felt good, too. I was in my zone, man. Damn, I might see Laurie today at school. She's pretty as fuck. Dude, I hope I do run into her.

"Hey, Jamari, huh..." said Steve, with his hand reached towards mine, with the blunt in his hand. I was in my own world for a little bit. I grabbed the blunt and I placed my lips on the weed-filled cigar as gently as possible. I inhaled as soft as possible but that was all it took for my chest to be filled with smoke. I was now coughing and choking with smoke coming out of my mouth. It wasn't like this the first time. I felt like I was about to die. The cold weather made the air so thin, it made it harder to breathe. I ended up spitting everywhere and I almost threw up but because I didn't eat yet, I couldn't throw up.

Steve, Lance, and Jacob were laughing their asses off. I was so ashamed, I wanted to run away. These dudes were laughing at my misery. Luckily Lance had a bottle of water in his backpack. When he gave me the water, I was so relieved. It felt like an angel landed on my head. I drank the water like a mad man lost in the desert.

All of the winter chills I had went out of the window. I was now a chimney, hot while letting out smoke. When my mini-episode stopped, I stood there, watching the white boys smoke dope. They inhaled and exhaled effortlessly and I was kind of jealous at the fact that I'm not cool enough to do that. Thinking about it, I'm not cool enough to do anything. Seems like I only live life through a dream.

Now I have a blurry vision, I think I have just seen a pigeon. Oh shit, man. Now I'm really tripping. My eyes are really heavy right now. I looked up at the street and I could see waves, the kind you see when you glare at the horizon on a sunny day. My head feels like it's filled with clouds. I guess this is how being high feels like. Standing still in the same position for like 5 minutes.

Chapter 10

Being high wasn't bad at all. I felt good after all of the coughing and stuff.

Steve and the other boys were smoking when Steve looked at me and said, "Hey, so what happened with you and Laurie? Did you bang her? She's such a fucking slut." Lance and Jacob started laughing but I didn't think that was funny. I resented the comment he made because I really like Laurie. She's more beautiful than most of the girls at school. Plus, I'm pleased with her style and demeanor. She is so fun to be around, she is nothing like Carmena but she's still a good person to me. Since I didn't want to sound like a punk, I replied, "Yeah, I fucked that bitch in her car."

"Wow, bro. Was it good? They say she got good pussy." "It was alright."

Steve shrugged his shoulders and laughed, he said he was on his way to school. I shook the three musketeers' hands and watched them walk away. I figured if I was seen walking with them, it would seem suspicious, so I waited in the back. I'm still kind of in my feelings about what Steve said. Laurie is a cool girl. She didn't give me that slutty vibe. Damn, I can't make her my girlfriend if people think she's a slut. I don't want to be the guy that marries the chick every guy is screwing. I want a girl that will make me feel special as if I were the only guy in the world. I want a girl that is special. Someone that won't give it up to just anybody.

To me, a woman is a special thing. As my dad would say, "A man that has a wife has a good thing." I believe love is the most powerful thing in the world. Love is the reason why I'm living today, There is nothing stronger than the love between man and woman. I want to be loved and in love. That would give my life a purpose. You can be the most wealthy guy on the planet but if no one loves you, then you're poor. Imagine how our world would be like if we didn't love. We would be animals just reproducing because of primitive urges. The beauty of love fills the world with joy.

I see women as delicate beings. Life is so short, man, why not spend all of the time you're on earth in love with the people you love? What can be better than that? Nothing. I assume love is the only thing a person really needs. Well, that, food, and water.

Wondering, is it really possible for me to find love? Even if I find love, will I keep it? Will it last? Unexpected things happen all the time. What if the person I'm loving is in love with someone else and leaves me? I don't think I can handle another heartbreak. My heart still is nowhere near healed. Carmena was perfect for me. She was the one for me. I loved her so much. She was so amazing. Carmena was so intelligent. They don't make many like that anymore. So what, she made a mistake. Carmena, it was a mistake. You didn't have to kill yourself with drugs. I forgive you. Please come back to me. The tears slowly rolling down my cheek but turned to ice because of the weather. I can't even cry without that going wrong.

I should make my way to school now that the coast is clear. When I started walking, all I could do was think about Carmena. Things aren't going my way, but if I can talk to Laurie, I might feel a little better in this time of despair. She might be able to lift weight off of my heavy heart. Hopefully. But for now, I have to walk around with my self-pity.

As I began to approach the school, I saw kids walking with backpacks. I saw students exiting their parent's cars and closing the door, then head for the main school entrance. There were like 30 cars out front. The street was cluttered with big trucks, SUVs, and the occasional four-door sedan. It was warming to see all of the concerned parents taking their children to school.

I saw this one girl get out of one of the big trucks, dressed in pajamas and slippers. Her parents must be blind. I would never let my daughter step out of the house like that. Then again, her parents are probably just some kids that had a kid when they were kids. I saw another kid walking in bog cowboy boots, jeans, and jacket. I immediately called him a redneck which was wrong but still, he is a country boy.

I saw a few students driving their own cars to school, which I imagine must be the coolest feeling ever. Being able to jump in a car and go anywhere you please. If I owned a car, I would just drive straight and don't look back. I would go far away from here to escape this empty town that's filled with people so stuck in their ways they suck the life out of this place.

Then again, running away wouldn't solve any of my problems. Regardless of how many miles I drive away, I still have to depart with my broken heart. That goes everywhere I go.

When I walked into the school, I got an adrenaline rush but it went away after 30 seconds. Then I felt like I had to take a shit, so I went to the restroom. I entered the restroom and thought to myself, this place is surprisingly clean. Back home, the bathroom would have filthy condoms and toilet paper on the floor and stuff. I sat on the toilet and the urge to defecate was soon gone. So I pissed and went to wash my hands. That's when I realized I had a bigger problem on my hands. I looked in the mirror and my eyes were bloodshot red. Oh shit, I'm fucked, I thought to myself. What the fuck am I going to do? That's when I decided to wash my face one thousand times, hoping the water would clear my eyes.

That was a total failure. The only benefit from that was, my face was now squeaky clean. After I refreshed myself with the smooth feeling of water touching my face, I took off for class, unafraid of the consequences. The weed gave me a sort of I don't give a fuck feeling. Whatever happens, happens. Fuck it.

While I'm walking to class, this tall white kid with black hair, brown eyes, blue shirt, blue jeans, and cowboy boots bumps into me. I bumped him pretty hard. I was walking really fast but I didn't notice until I bumped him. I apologized to him and everything but he gave me this stink face. I have seen that face before. It means, I would stomp on you but you apologized already. I felt kind of bad for bumping into him.

Now I was walking around all extra cautious, hoping I don't crash my car into someone else. I'm also happy the kid didn't want to fight. Back home, dudes fought about that stupid shit. Bumping someone or stepping on someone's shoes could end your life where I'm from. In Miami, tension is always in the air. You never know when it's going to go down. That's why I stay out of people's way. That's also why schools back home had security guards and policemen around 24/7. School over here is sweet, man. I don't have to worry about being harassed because I'm poor. I don't have to be afraid of being myself. Well, I take that back. I don't have to be scared of my race but I do have to be conscious of my surroundings.

I made it to class right when the school bell rang. I went to my seat and didn't really give anyone any attention. My teacher looked at me like she wanted to say something but she just continued teaching. I sat in my seat, just thinking about life and the obstacles I will face later on.

My life has changed forever and for some reason, I felt like it's slipping away from me. The worst part is I feel I can't get it back. What can I do? Who knows what the future may hold? But I do know I control today and I will make the best of today, every day. By the time I made up my mind to do my classwork, class was finished.

I got up, walked out of class, not giving a fuck if I turned in my assignment or not. I repeated this same pattern until it was lunchtime. Normally, I wouldn't eat anything for lunch but I'm more hungry than a stray dog. What they say is that weed gives you the munchies. Aww, man. My belly is growling like a purse dog. While I'm standing in the lunch line, I take a brief look to my left and I see Kerry and Keylina sitting at the table. I couldn't help but think to myself, Keylina is beyond pretty, she is sumptuous.

Chapter 11

Keylina looks so tasty, I could just eat her right now. I kept looking to my left in the line until I got my tray and sat with my friends. "Hey, Kerry. What's going on, Keylina?"

"Hey, how are you?" Kerry replied while Keylina stayed silent. "I'm doing good. I'm just hungry today."

"I can see that. I don't remember the last time I saw you eat." "Yeah, I have to start eating more. The food isn't even that bad." "Hmm. Y'all Miami boy too good to eat school lunch?"

"Nah, I ain't say that. Normally, I don't feel like eating."

"I guess, boy." Kerry made me smile with her attitude. It reminded me of girls back home. She brightened my day. I have been feeling smug all day. Between her and these chicken nuggets, I don't know what made me happier. The only thing that is bothering me at this moment is Keylina's silence. She seems irritated, something must be on her mind. She has yet to take a bite of her food. I would ask her for her chicken nuggets but that wouldn't seem very cool at all. She would most likely lose interest in me if I did that. Who am I kidding? A girl like her wouldn't see a thing in me. Looking at her sit there with something on her mind was eating me up on the inside. I had to say something, so I did.

"Keylina, what's up? You okay? You ain't said nothing all day." She gave me a mean look and hesitated to speak but said, "I'm doing fine, Jamari."

"You sure? You didn't try to eat none of your food." "I'm not hungry I guess..."

"I feel the same way sometimes."

"Oh. So what happened to you earlier this week?" That question was unexpected. I was not prepared for that.

"I didn't know what to say, so I stuttered before I lied and said, I was suffering from insomnia. I didn't sleep for 3 whole days, so I fell out in class. My body just broke down."

"Umm-hmm. You was probably out all night with that Laurie girl." I got caught off guard by another blow but this one was more fatal than the first. When she said that, I got defensive and nervous at the same time. I have a crush on Keylina and I don't want to ruin my shot with her because of Laurie, so I responded in the only way I knew how, just flat out denying the whole thing.

"I don't know what you talking about."

"Boy, don't act like you stupid. What you and Laurie got going on?" "Uhhh...

"Everybody knows already. What you lying for?" "Everybody know what?"

"That y'all left Steve's party together to go have sex."

I was dumbfounded by how much she knew and by how quickly word travels around. This is a tough spot to be in because there is nothing I can say. I'm so nervous at this point, I can feel my deodorant coming off. My stomach is going in circles like a dog chasing its tail. "Who told you this?"

"Don't worry about it. Just know I know," Keylina said, then shook her head, waved her hand, and rolled her eyes.

Just when I thought it was over, Kerry jumped in. "Which Laurie you talking about, girl?"

"Laurie Scwan. The one on the softball team."

"Eww. You talking about the one that dated Josh Norman." "Yeah, her."

"Uh uh boy, why you messing with her? She ain't no good."

I'm just sitting there staring at them, flustered. They pushed all of my buttons just now. The one day I decided to be friendly and talk to people, the shit backfire on me. I just stayed silent with a disturbed look on my face, while Kerry and Keylina went back and forth until the bell rang. I was rescued by the bell. When the bell went off, I was happy to get up and leave. As much as I enjoy being around Keylina, today's conversation was beyond awkward, it was torture.

"Alright, y'all. I'll catch y'all another time." Kerry replied, "Okay, bye."

Keylina looked at me and said, "So, you not going to answer my question?" "Nah man, what you talking about?"

"Boy, bye..." "Alright."

"So, you not going to give me a hug?"

I was shocked when she said that. I have been fumbling all day, so instead of messing this one up, I just hugged her. Keylina is shorter than me, so when I hugged her I was looking down on her. I could see the straight line in the middle of her parted head. When my skin touched hers, she had a very pleasant scent. Keylina smelled awesome. I felt like I was in paradise for the few seconds I was hugging her. The world around didn't exist for a little while. It was time to let her go, so I backed up but she was still holding me tight. When she released me, she gazed up at me. By this time, we were face to face, so I kissed her. I didn't think about it. Kissing her was the right thing to do. After being seduced by her lovely face, I had no choice. Kissing her was compelling. It was like two planets crashing into each other in a distant universe.

The wet kiss lasted for a few seconds before coming to a gradual end. I sensed she wanted to continue kissing but we were still in the lunchroom and we had to go to class. I looked at her surprised but confidently said, "See you later, Keylina."

She smiled, let off a small giggle, and replied, "Bye, Jarnari," then I noticed Kerry looking appalled as if she and Keylina never spoke about this before.

Kerry said, "Aww, look at y'all. Y'all look so cute together."

I brushed it off and said I got to get to class while Keylina said, "Stop girl, you play too much.

I said my last goodbyes and that was it. I walked away with the biggest smile on my face. I can't believe I kissed Keylina and she didn't stop me or nothing. I was happier than a kid in a toy store, high off the atmosphere. I kept replaying that singular instance in my head over and over. I'm still confused as to how all this happened but the only conclusion I can come to is, whenever I get the chicks to flock to me, I don't know if it's the drugs that's giving me a confidence boost or what, but I love the way how I'm feeling today. I like this getting high thing, it's not bad.

I floated all the way to class, the kiss uplifted my spirit. I sat in class and daydreamed the whole time about Keylina. I couldn't wait to see her again. Her lips were soft and juicy. I adored every moment of it. Keylina is super beautiful. She was blessed by the gods. They took extra time when creating her. I was thinking about her so much when the teacher called on me to read out loud, I blurted out Keylina's name. Then I caught myself and asked what page number we were on because my book wasn't open.

I looked to my left and got the page number from my classmate. When I was prepared to read, the teacher called on someone else because I was slowing the class down. Cool, no problem with me. I didn't want to do shit anyways. I tried to focus on my classwork but my mind was blown. I had to be in a parallel universe. There is no way this happened. Keylina must have been feeling me all of this time. I would have never known if she didn't ask me for a hug. The only thing I'm wondering at this point is, how do you know when a chick likes you?

I'll look that up on Youtube or something when I get home. The internet has all the answers nowadays, but then again, some of the information you read online are unreliable.

I wish I had someone I could talk to about these types of situations. If I had friends, they could have led me in the right direction. I'm stuck, but that isn't important right now. I know Keylina likes me. The real question is, how do I move forward after this? We kissed, hugged, and we talk often. Damn, I'm in need of some advice. Maybe Jamesha will be able to help me with this. Nah, I ain't going to say nothing to her. I don't want her all in my business.

The school bell rang and my mind quickly shifted away from Keylina. I was now focused on my way back home in the snow. Walking home wasn't a problem for me but thinking about it was. The weather reminds me of how far I've come. All the way from the '30s to the '70s. That's a big difference, from tank tops and swimming trunks to thermal jackets with leather boots. Still, I have to brace myself for that wind chill, it ain't no joke.

I made it out front next to the main entrance and I zipped up my jacket, tied up my boots, and placed my hands in my pockets. When I walked out front, it was more packed than this morning. You know, the usual I guess. Rich kids jumping in cars and the less fortunate walking home.

Back home, when I would walk home, there would be at least 5 of us taking the same route. We would walk together in the morning and after school. We used to meet up like clockwork at the same place and same time every day. Looking back now, I relish those childhood memories with my little brother. We used to go everywhere together. People come and go but memories last forever. That's one thing this cold world can't take from you;

memories. Sometimes I feel like I was dealt a bad hand, like the circumstance in which I was raised. I feel as if I am bound to lose, no matter what, as a black man. Now that Donald Trump is President, things are worse. White supremacist neo-Nazis are rallying and protesting and our POTUS is calling them fine people. How can I win? I have to live with the fact that as a colored man, I have a target on my back. People of my color are being gunned down and stored in prisons until they expire. When I leave my home, there's a chance I might not come back home due to being a black man. I'm always at risk.

The police can harass me at any given moment and I can't do anything about it. The country we live in was founded on the genocide of the Native Americans and the slavery of colored people. The most horrifying part about it is people are forgetting the past, so there's a possibility history might repeat itself. Who knows what will happen with Trump as the head of our fragile country?

Walking home, I felt like I was retracing my steps in the snow. I was reliving this morning and all the emotions as I walked through the skate park. Laughing at myself because I almost killed myself smoking. Aww man, I wonder when I will smoke again. I don't need the stuff anyways.

I crossed the street and left the skate park. 10 minutes later, I was at the front door of my home. Knocking, waiting for someone to open the door. Click Clack. The sound of the door unlocking startled me a little bit. Behind the door was my sister's husband, drunker than the village idiot on New Year's Eve. The look on his face disgusted me. For some reason, every time he sees me, he looks displeased. You could smell the alcohol on his breath as soon as he opened the door. His eyes were red like a broken traffic light. Instead of displaying my frustration, I chose to be a bigger person and said, "Hey man, what's up?" "Shut the fuck up. Why you always stressing

Jamesha out? You didn't have to go to school, why didn't you just stay home?"

"I have to get my education to become somebody in this world."

"Wake up, lil' nigga! Wake up! You're just another nigga. The white man's education won't do shit for you."

I stayed mute, fearing I would add more fuel to the fire if I challenged his ignorance, I turned my back to him and headed to my quarters.

He continued his drunk man rant stating, "Don't walk away from me, nigga. Keep on going to them white folks' school, they gon' kill your black ass should they find out you messing with them white girls."

Although most of his words were said with a slur, the last sentence slapped me in the face. I found it ridiculous how ignorant he is but still, his words had some kind of truth to it. Here and now, most of the world is open to the idea of whites and blacks dating. Still, some people despise interracial couples and most of these people seem like they live in North Dakota. Donald Trump won North Dakota with a 98% vote. That says a lot about the inhabitants of this land.

I entered my room and laid down on the bed, after a do-nothing day at school. My bed felt so good after that walk home. I took my boots and jacket off. My bed never felt any better.

I fell asleep shortly after I laid down, then I had this bizarre dream about a little boy chasing a shadow around. At first, he didn't notice the shadow behind him but once he did, he followed it everywhere. The shadow led the boy to an abandoned home and inside the house was a man sleeping. The man appeared to be homeless, but once the boy walked in, the man woke up and showed the boy a handful of gold. The gold was so shiny that the shadow disappeared. The homeless man then was about to speak but I woke up.

I was puzzled. I didn't know what the dream meant but I was scared of it for some reason. My mouth was dry and I was more thirsty than a lion at a river. I got up to get a drink of water from the kitchen.

The hallways were dark, all the lights were off but there was light at the end of the tunnel. I walked into the living room. The TV was on and my nephews were sleeping. They fell asleep playing video games. I chuckled and went to get my glass of water. I crept into the kitchen, hoping not to make noise to awaken the children. I got my drink, then I turned off the TV and slowly crept back to the other end of the tunnel.

My life is kind of like a tunnel, a never-ending darkness. The light is at the end of it. I will be happy when I die - when I exit the tunnel.

I got into my room and threw myself on my bed. I was laying down on my bed, staring in the dark. I did that until I fell asleep again. I had a series of dreams but I didn't remember because no incredible event took place.

Then I had one more dream. It was about me. I was at my house in Miami and my little brother Jamal was running around causing trouble, like usual. I remember yelling at him and stuff, then he started crying. When he started crying, I began to feel guilty for yelling at him, so I apologized and said, "It's okay, little bro. I miss you so much. I love you, Jamal."

He replied, "I love you, too," and gave me a hug. I was so happy to be with my little brother, it was as if I forgot he passed away. I'm hugging him and it felt like I was defying all the laws of life. I was talking and holding a dead man, my baby brother. I was baffled but also eager to hear from Jamal. It's been a long time since I saw him. While I'm talking to Jamal, my mom yells, "Someone is knocking on the door!" I told Jamal I will be right back and headed towards the front of the house. This seemed kind of odd to me, no one ever came to my house. When I answered the door, to my surprise, it was the love of my life, Carmena. She looked spectacular with her beautiful light brown skin and her long natural black hair. I said, "Hi, Carmena," and hugged her. After we greeted each other, I insisted that she come inside. We went to my room where we began to kiss and touch each other passionately. Her presence sparked a fire within me. I was extremely pleased to see her. Seeing her burned away all my pain and bitterness. We were on my bed kissing. When she decided to take her shirt off, I was kind of nervous but I been waiting for this moment. Her breasts were beautiful, she doesn't have big breasts but they are a good size for a petite woman such as herself.

I started taking my clothes off, then we were both fully naked. I kissed her neck and sucked on her milky breast. The sex concept is still foreign to me. I never had any, so I was scared to start. That's when she pushed me and grabbed my penis and sucked it. The feeling was indescribable but it was gratifying. All I could do was make faces and sounds while she sucked my soul away.

Then Jamal ran in the room and scared the shit out of us. We both reached for the covers and got under them. I was furious and embarrassed. Then I woke up. When I woke up, there was light coming out of the window and frost on the other side. I looked around for my phone to call Carmena and tell her how much I love her, only to realize that was impossible; she had passed away. I felt so crestfallen. Two minutes prior, I was just at the top of the world. Now I'm back, falling in the bottomless pit.

When I got up, I had a major erection. I reached down to feel myself and felt moisture. It was a slime-like substance. Then it hit me; I came on myself.

Chapter 12

Me being me, I had to touch and smell it. This was new to me. I didn't know I could release like this while in my sleep. When I smelled the clear sticky substance, I noticed the scent wasn't the best but it wasn't that bad. The aroma was similar to sweat mixed with something else. I was going to taste it but I figured that would be disgusting, weird, and a little gay. I'm not saying I have anything against gay people but doing that seemed like the wrong thing to do.

I'm laying down in my bed with a rock hard erection and sperm all over my boxers, thinking about how is it possible for me to cum while sleeping. Then I thought about Carmena and felt my heart drop. My first time making love was an illusion, a dream, a fictional reality. I was in such a good place, now I'm back on this astral plane. Carmena and I had a lot of good times together and although she is no longer here, she still brings me joy. I didn't want to push her for sex or force her to do something she was uncomfortable doing. Now I wish we had sex and had a kid so I could have the child to remember her by. I miss my wife a lot, only if I could have her back.

I miss Jamal too. Seeing my brother was dope. It's been a long time and still, the connection is there. My dream felt so real, it's as if I was in another dimension. I guess I have to start getting more sleep so I could spend more time with my loved ones. Knowing that the only way I could see Carmena and Jamal again was through a dream, forced tears burst out my eyes.

Early in the morning, and my day began as dark as night. I laid in my bed of self-pity for about an hour, then I decided to get up. I had to wash this semen off me and start my day.

I showered, brushed my teeth, and did my entire morning routine. I was about to exit the bathroom when I caught something in the mirror. I thought

I saw someone behind me in the mirror but it was just my dreadlocks. I was analyzing myself in the mirror, only to be appalled at the discovery of this new man I saw. When you look in the mirror, you're supposed to see your reflection but I saw someone I had never seen before. I faced the mirror and said, "Who are you?" only to see this man reply with the very same question.

I'm done. My life is over. I looked at the razor blade laying on the neck of the sink. I contemplated killing myself. I have nothing to live for, why not? My wife is gone, my brother is gone. I might as well cross over to the other side and join them. I picked up the blade but I set it right back down. I was too afraid to do it.

I broke down and sat on the bathroom floor, crying at the sight of the man in the mirror. The guy that is such a fuck up he can't even kill himself. Life is deep, it's big, it's vast, but you only live life once and the man in the mirror knew that much.

I spent the whole weekend in an emotional slump in my room, staring at the walls. My sister came in and checked on me every now and then but that was it. The highlight of the weekend was when my nephews would come into the room, yelling and screaming, playing with one another. Things like that made me smile but also kind of sad. It reminds me of my brother and I in our younger days. Back when life didn't have any worries. I'm 17 now and it seems like I got nothing to live for but I got so much to live for. There are plenty of things I haven't experienced yet. I hope I live to see it all.

Overall, my weekend was boring and I was happy to be going to school. I got used to my medication, it really works too. When I take it, all the pain goes away. It's like I'm numb to all the bullshit. I may have some sad thoughts, but the pain isn't as strong anymore.

I was walking through the hallway at school after asking to use the restroom. As I was on my way, I saw two kids and they gave me a funny look. No problem, the usual.

I entered the restroom and went to use the urinal. After I urinated, I washed my hands and walked out. As soon as I walked out, I saw Laurie roaming the hallways. Her back was turned to me but I knew that was her. I called her name one time, softly. It was so soft she couldn't hear. I raised my voice and called for a second time, still no response. So I walked up on her and said, "Hey, Laurie."

"OMG, hi Jamari." "What you up to?"

"Nothing, I'm just on my way to class." "What class do you have right now?" "Algebra 2."

"Oh, well I got history class right now." "You have Mr. Klein."

"Yeah, him. He's a pretty cool teacher." "Yeah, I had him last year."

"So, Laurie, what have you been up to lately?"

"Nothing really. Just been studying and going to work."

"That's cool. Well, I know you got to get to class, so I will catch up with you another time."

"Jamari, wait," she pulls out her phone, then she says, "What's your number?"

"Uhh, I remember now. 704-223-8808." "I'm going to text you."

"Alright." I reached in and hugged her, then she gave me a quick pop kiss. All of that happened kind of fast. I went to use the restroom and I got a kiss from Laurie. I mean, Laurie is very pretty. I can't deny my attraction to her. My confidence is through the roof after that kiss.

After I walked her to class, I noticed there was this kid who seemed to be following me, but I hadn't noticed until I turned around to go to my class.

It was strange, but then again, I'm in North Dakota, people do weird shit all the time. I just need to worry about myself.

I got into class on my horse and rode to my seat. Laurie made me so happy, I was in space. My body was in class but my mind was somewhere else. I was thankful for that because the class was getting a bit stressful. White kids don't understand "black history month". They feel as if this knowledge doesn't apply to them and is not a part of their history when it is a major part of U.S. history and world history. The United States of America was built by the deaths of millions of slaves and their hard work. The blood, sweat, and tears black folk sacrificed made this country. People were being held captive and they were being sold at auctions. They were tortured; the women were raped and fathers were killed. They came to America on massive sized boats and starved for weeks. Families were separated, wives and husbands, mothers and kids separated to be sold as slaves. All of this because they were deemed incompetent because of the lifestyle they felt comfortable living. Because they were black skin-colored, they were not considered people. Discriminated, murdered, imprisoned, still, that is the fate of the black man in America. Why? Because here we are 300 years later and we have ignorant people not willing to learn about the history of their own country. This goes for both black and white. Whites feel black history doesn't apply to them. Blacks feel like the history doesn't apply to them. When all the signs of today show it all. The system was made for us to fail, they never wanted us.

How could I raise a child in this world? The most heartbreaking thing is, one day, every black parent in America has to tell their child they will be denied some opportunities because they are black, which is sad but what can you do when you're 3/5 of a man? Your word doesn't have much value. We are not men, we are property.

I sat in class, thinking about my fate as a black man. I was doomed from the start. My thoughts were going back and forth from Malcolm X to MLK Future and Drake to The Weekend.

I loved the fact that I got a kiss from Laurie but I hated my circumstances. One of the only black kids in the whole school. I was an outcast, an outsider, and an alien.

The bell rang. Class was over but I was in such deep thought I sat there. I didn't notice the class was let out until my teacher said something, "Don't worry about it, kid. You're smart, you'll be fine."

"I replied, "Thank you," and got all my stuff and walked out of class, shaking my head. I was trying to make the blood flow through my body and wake me up.

I look around the hallway and I see kids all packed and bunched up. It was at least 3 cliques in the hallway, "The cowboys", "The Ball Players", and "The Stoners". The group of groupie chicks was around too. I didn't pay them any mind but the only thing was, the passageway seemed more cluttered than usual. I was kind of curious as to what was going on but I was always told to mind my business, so I did.

I'm walking and all I hear is voices everywhere. The hall got extremely loud, then I heard a cry from afar, "Nooo! Matt! Nooo!"

Then the whole place got silent and I got punched in the back of the head. I grabbed my head and turned around and received two more blows to the face before I realized what was happening.

Chapter 13

I was in a fight. I was being attacked. I took my bookbag off and squared up with the guy. The guy kind of dazed me with the first three sucker punches but I couldn't feel it. I was in go mode.

The brown hair, tall, skinny white boy with braids named Matt, from the school's basketball team decided he would fight, for what, the world may never know. That didn't matter now anyways, I had to fight this big motherfucker. I leaned in and threw a punch and it connected, but he hit me right back with a jab. He hit me good too, right in the jaw. We exchanged punches for good 30 seconds, then I bent over and grabbed him by the ankles and slammed him. A little wrestling trick I was taught. Growing up in Miami, you had to protect yourself and play fighting was a way of life back home.

I took him down, got on top of him, and punched him 6 times in the face. As I was hitting him, I started to feel good. Finally, a black man was winning something in this white man world. Then it dawned on me, I'm beating this white boy senseless in front of this crowd of kids, they might jump on my head.

The worse part of all was, I'm in school. I'm going to get suspended for this. I thought of this and felt remorseful. I looked down on the kid and clapped his face one last time and tried to get up. It was too late to quit, then teachers ran out of class and body slammed me and restrained me like a runaway slave.

The principal came up and it was a huge scene. Everything was silent until the teachers came. I blacked out for the most part. Now it was time to face the consequences of my actions.

Blood was everywhere. You would have thought we were on the West Coast. The floor looked like a freak accident happened. I looked at Matt's face and he was red and blue like the Haitian flag. I fucked him up bad. His face looked like a bruised tomato. I was excited to see how badly I messed this guy up. Back home, if you got into a fight and won, you was the man.

Everyone respected you. I can only imagine how much these people will respect me now, seeing I just beat this guy's ass, I know they won't fuck with me no more. Now I have to go to the principal's office and get my sentence. I will say on my behalf, so I won't get suspended for too long, that he started the fight and I was defending myself. Plus, I will throw the race card out there so I can get off scot-free. Hopefully, this will work.

I got into the Principal's office and he didn't say a word to me. He just typed away on his computer, filing the proper paperwork. My head was pounding and I'm dying to say my side of the story. I looked at him and said, "He hit me first. I was on my way to class. He started a fight with me because I'm black."

The Principle stared at me with demon eyes of fire and said, "I worked here 10 years and no fight happened until you got here. Listen here, you nigga boy, don't you say one more word while you in here."

I sat there scared as hell and in disbelief. This white man just called me a "nigga". The word means nothing when a black man says it but when a white guy says it, the game changes.

"You broke that boy's jaw and gave him a black eye and bruised him up real good. I got something for you."

I stayed there while he called my sister and told her to come pick me up.

I was suspended for 10 days.

I was crushed by the 10-day suspension. I won't see Laurie or Keylina for two whole weeks. This sucks, and I fucked up my record. No college will take me now. My sister is going to chew me out when she comes.

While I'm preparing the sob story for my sister, the bell rings and school lets out. I wanted to leave but the Principal wouldn't let me.

Two policemen walked in the office and my heart sunk deep under the earth's crust. I was going to jail. My heart was beating uncontrollably. I felt like I was going to have a heart attack. The only funny thing is, no matter where you go, all cops look the same.

These dickheads were the typical cop boys. One was 6'2, black hair, brown eyes, and really big, like he works out every day. The other one was 5'10 and had a bald spot in the middle of his head. He looked like the kind of cop you saw eating doughnuts with coffee. They came in and said, "This is him."

"Yeah."

"Okay, give me all his information."

I was about to shit on myself. I'm going to jail. I can't believe it. Over a fight I didn't even start? Come on, WTF? What am I supposed to do, just let him beat me up?

I was handcuffed real tight, so my wrists were hurting. I'm walking out of school with my head down, ashamed of myself, being escorted to the cops' car. The main entrance was full of people and police everywhere. You would have thought I murdered somebody. Parents, students, and local residents. Everyone was out. I became terrified. These people are out here because they want to kill me. The cops might not be able to protect me.

When I walked out of the double doors, the noise became vivid. They were chanting in protest of my existence. The crowd said, "Make America great again, make black people slaves again."

Shocked at the discovery of the truth, the world is exactly the way how people say it is. Against the black man. Honestly, I didn't think it was legal for people to say something like that.

They all had their phones, signs, and everything out. I couldn't understand how things escalated this fast. It was just a fight. Something this big is uncalled for. I didn't plan on whipping that boy today. I guess the truth won't hide itself no more. The people of North Dakota no longer want to share their home with black people unless we were servants. I entered the back seat of the cop car safe. Thankful that mob of people didn't kill me. Sad to know I'm grateful to be in a cop car. I looked in the back window and saw the mob going crazy. The trucks were all out. I'm guessing they are going to follow us.

Everything feels like deja vu, like I had seen this before. I just can't quite put my name on it. I wonder what my mom is going to say? What is my sister going to do? How am I going to get out? Shit. What am I going to do?

I was riding in the cop car for 10 minutes when we came to a stop at the county jail. The jail was not that far away. I passed by it a few times in the car with my sister. The building didn't look like a jail. It looked like more of a banker building.

The cop stopped in front of an automatic gate. The gate slid open and he drove slowly in the parking lot. Squad cars filled the lot along with unmarked cars. Funny how the police ride in the same cars as regular civilians. There is nothing the government won't do to invade our privacy. Our society is a fraud. America is the opposite of what it claims to be. The land of the free or the home of corporate slavery.

I got out of the car with my bodyguards. I got searched one more time before entering the building. This time I was disgusted by the way I was being handled. The guy touched my balls and my ass. That shook me up. I felt violated and uncomfortable. When I got in, two other guys were being booked. They both were homeless guys that came to jail on purpose to beat the weather. These guys were junkies on crack and meth, most likely. It was almost heart ripping to see humans looking like them.

During the booking process, I got on a scale and they measured my weight, took my height, and asked me if I had any problems mentally. I said no. Now it was time for me to go through this door. The holding cells were on the other side of here. They took all my stuff and gave me some shower shoes.

I'm curious to see what awaits me on the other side of the door. It just might be life or death. When I got on the other side, there was a TV and 5 rows of chairs with 2 guys in each row. There was a camera for me to take my mug shot. The two junkies before me come to jail so much, they didn't take their photos. They used one from their previous stay at this luxurious hotel. I took my mug shot and I looked like I don't know what.

I was told to go to a back room. When I got there, a man with blue gloves looked at me and handed me a set of orange clothes, the classic jail look. Before I was allowed to put the clothes on, I had to be naked. I felt degraded being strip search while another man inspected my body. The worse part was the squat and cough. I did it, then the guard looked at me and said, "Spread them."

I looked at him, unsure of what he meant. Then he said, "Spread them cheeks." I have never been so embarrassed in my life. I had to spread my butt cheeks for this guy who seemed to get a kick out of this.

Chapter 14

When I got to the housing unit some hours later, I felt sick. The place was kind of big, upstairs and downstairs. There were about 30 cells on each floor. Two small TVs were in the unit; one for whites and the other for Hispanics. Well, that's what I'm guessing, because I saw white boys on one side and the Spanish-looking guys on the other.

The officer handed me a small bag with a comb, toothbrush, toothpaste, deodorant, and soap. He also gave me two white sheets and a blanket. I guess this is what the State of North Dakota is required to give me. After he gave me those items, he pointed towards cell 0052. I guess that's where I was supposed to go. I walked to my cell, cautious of the fact that I was the only black guy in the dorm.

I got in my cell and saw a toilet, a sink, a small window, and a bunk bed. The floor was dusty, as though it had never been cleaned before. Trash wrappers were all over the floor. The place was filthy. The bottom bunk was made up, so I guessed someone slept there. I fixed my bed on the top bunk. Once it was made, I got on top and laid down. As soon as I closed my eyes, I heard the door open and I jumped up.

An Indian man walked in. He had long gray hair, all the way down to his back, with a big gray beard to match. He was skinny and really old. The man greeted me with a smile. "Hey, youngster. How are you?"

I replied reluctantly, "I'm fine, and you?"

"I'm doing lovely, I'm alive. So, what you in here for?" "Assault. What about you?"

"Animal cruelty."

"How did you get caught doing that?"

"It was for religious purposes. I don't care. I should be going home soon anyway. 10 months here, only one more to go."

"That's a long time, I don't know how you did it. I would have gone crazy." "How you know I ain't crazy?"

"Uhhh...

"I'm just kidding with you, buddy." I started laughing, then he said, "So, Jamari, what are you going to do?"

"I don't know. I have to call my sister, I guess... Wait, how did you know my name?"

"I'm looking suspicious at this guy at this point, then he states, "Your arrest form is right here on the floor, that's why."

"Oh, my bad man. I didn't mean to offend you."

"Don't worry kid. You have a lot more serious stuff coming ahead. Well, look here, don't talk to any white dude in here, they all want to kill you. Secondly, don't talk to any Mexicans, they all want to fuck you. And third of all, only leave this room to shower and use the phone. Don't watch TV People get killed over those TVs"

I was frightened by what he said even though I already knew that I was a target. It just seemed unreal to me how quickly prison culture became my reality. I nodded my head and said, "Okay." All the juices were all stirred up in my stomach and ready to explode. I asked the Indian guy if I could use the restroom, and he said, "Yeah, no problem. Just let me know before you go so I can cover up my face."

"Alright." I used the filthy toilet while the guy sat there on the bed with his face wrapped with white sheets. I had to go, so it all came out pretty fast. The room was smelly when I got done with it. After that, I felt just a little bit better but I was still uncomfortable.

I got up on my bunk and laid down until I fell asleep. I had a dream about a mob of people protesting with tiki torches and signs. They were outside of a church, and inside the church, a funeral service was going on. I wasn't in this dream for some reason. I was like God or something, looking down on all the madness going on earth. People were crying quietly in the church, while this one baby was crying hysterically. The baby was so loud the family was embarrassed but no one said a thing. They let the baby scream for minutes. Meanwhile, on the outside, a crowd of white folk was ready to set the church on fire. The people were shouting and in rage. You could see the anger on their faces. They all were chanting, "Make America great again, make black people slaves again," with their torches in their hands. Then a fight broke out among those in the crowd and the street was in total chaos. Police were everywhere but there were so many people, they had little effect on the mob of people. The last thing I could remember was a car driving into the crowd of people and gunshots going off. People died for sure, I know it.

When I woke up, there were two trays of food on the counter by the sink. It was still dark out, so it had to be around 5 or 6 in the morning. My cellmate handed me my tray and I looked at it, and I got sad; the food was garbage. A piece of bologna, bread, jelly, and scrambled eggs that smelled like fart. I didn't want to eat it but I had no choice. I hadn't eaten since yesterday. After I ate, I laid down on my bed until I fell asleep again. Then after two hours, I woke up and had to go to court for my bond hearing.

The officer got me out of my cell. The man was huge; he was at least 6'1 and 250 pounds. The guy seemed to have a military swagger to him. The way he walked, talked, and looked. I'm still tired from barely sleeping. I got handcuffed and shackled around my feet. The only thing I could imagine was, if I'm being treated like this just for a fight at school, I could only imagine how they treated murderers.

Prison is no place for a human. It's disgusting, man. Rats and roaches running around everywhere, the food is horrible. I don't know how these guys do it. While I was thinking of all this, the officer searched me and two other guys. The other guys looked like maniacs. Both had big beards, bald heads, and tattoos everywhere. By the looks of it, they were most likely brothers and co- defendants pending trial for the same case.

The officers walked us out of the housing unit, where we met up with 5 other inmates from another housing unit. The whole time I was going through this process, I was thinking, this place isn't for me. I'm too smart to be here. Once I get out, I won't ever come back because I know better now. What about all of the innocent men in prisons all over the world. These places shouldn't even exist, to be honest. Someone has to do something about this, because this ain't right.

When I arrived in court, I looked around. And just like in school, I'm in a room filled with white folk. I was seated on the left side of the judge, with the two junkies from yesterday. Their names were called before mine. The judge denied them bond because they repeated offenders for possession of meth. The guys seemed unbothered by the judge's decision.

Meanwhile, I was farting and sweating because I was uncertain of my outcome at this point. I can only be optimistic and hope for the best. The courtroom to me seemed messy like everything was all over the place.

My "attorney" had 5 clients, the judge looked off her game. The place was like a zoo to me. Papers being shuffled everywhere, inmates walking in and out of a secret back door. There were also family members crying in the stands, waiting to see their relative come back from the dead.

The District Attorney was a complete asshole. His job was to make every guy look like the biggest criminal on earth, while your public defender tries to put up a fight for you but they have so many clients and such limited information, it's hopeless. It was sad, man, to see how people could get lost in the system. Innocent till proven guilty or guilty till proven innocent? The DA makes everyone feel guilty to me. The judge read a paper, then said, "Where is Jamari Picard, number 15766-

"Right here," my lawyer replied. Then I stood up nervously, while my heart was beating violently.

The judge said, "Why the hell is he here? He's only 17. From what I'm reading, he is in custody for a fight at school. Two teenage boys fighting seems normal to me."

My lawyer stated, "Your honor, my client has no prior arrest record. He is just a boy. I am requesting you release on pre-trial release for a first time offender."

"Well, this is what I'm going to do; he will go home on pre-trial and the charges will be dropped."

"Thank you, your honor."

The gavel dropped and I just got the news, soon I will be a free man. I felt so good knowing that at least someone else knew that this was bullshit. The other thing is because I'm 17, I'm supposed to be in juvenile jail, not an adult correctional facility. I thought I was going to get slammed on top of my head. Wooo!

Now I have to head back to the unit until I'm released. I still have to be cautious. Even though I'm about to get out, I could still get stabbed at any moment.

On the way back to the housing unit, the officer looked at me and said, You lucky son of a bitch. If I was the judge, I would have locked up your ugly motherfucking ass so long you would forget your name."

I was going to say something but I just put my head down in shame. I could have jeopardized my freedom by replying to this bigot but it wasn't worth it. The judicial system in America is all messed up, man. It's built to see a young black man fail. By now, I was halfway back to the dorm. My feet were sore from the shackles. I'm pretty sure I will have blisters by tomorrow, but the pain wasn't anything. I took it in because I was going to be free pretty soon. Crazy how this guy was talking to me like I'm a criminal. That really bothered me, how people don't know anything about you but wish for you to go through pain.

I got to the housing unit but they didn't let me go in, they took me somewhere else. The brothers went back to the dorm. I'm guessing I'm going to be released. That's why they didn't let me back in the cell. The officers took me to a holding cell on the next floor. I sat down on a stainless steel bench. The room was cold and the bench felt like ice. I waited anxiously by myself, left only to wonder what will be my fate.

The officers walked into the room and uncuffed me. They made me take off all my clothes, then squat and cough. These moments for me were the worst; it felt wrong, taking off my clothes while grown men scrutinized me. Once I took all my clothes off, the officers started laughing at me. I was humiliated. At that moment, I felt nothing but rage about to consume me. Tears started rolling down my face as I reached for my boxers. Then one of the officers said, "You lucky we didn't tear that ass boy."

The other officer said, "I wouldn't dare stick my dick in a nigga ass." Two of the officers started laughing but the third guy gave me the impression that he didn't like what was going on. He was just the unlucky lower rank officer that had to do what his boss said. At least there are some people with some type of dignity in the world still.

The officers left the room and I put my clothes on, crying, praying for the end of this. When I made it to my cell, I got on my bunk and went to sleep. Then my celly, the Indian man named Abu Swiswi came in and asked me, "How'd it go at court?"

I told him, "I should be leaving any minute now on pre-trial release." "That's good, son. Now check this out. You were all over the news for beating that boy. People are protesting this case. They want you to get locked up. You need some protection, these people will try to kill you."

My mind was blown. I didn't think this was that serious. On the news for what? Oh shit, I'm fucked. These people are going to kill me.

"They are outside of the courthouse, protesting the fact that you will be released awaiting trial." I didn't know what to say, so I didn't say anything. "This is what I'm going to do for you. I'm going to give you my wife's address and phone number. Call her when you get out. She will do something for you."

"Okay, Abu. So what do I do now?"

"I'll pray for you but that's all I can do."

The room was silent for a while after he said that. The sound of keys dangling and doors being locked and unlocked filled my ear. Then another officer was at the door of my cell, telling me to pack all of my stuff. I didn't pack anything up. I just told Abu bye, then I left my cell ecstatically.

I had to sign a few papers out front, then I was on my route to the outtake holding cell. When I got to the cell, I was handed back my stuff. I was sort of happy about that. I had only been in jail for about a day and a half but it felt like forever.

The officer called my name, took my fingerprints, and my DNA, then I was walked through the exit of the jail. Every step towards the end felt more and more gratifying. I deserved my freedom. I should have never been deprived of my liberty in the first place anyways.

I was walking out of the prison with an I'm going to change the world attitude. When I got out of the building, the aroma of the free world made love to my nose. I wandered around, not knowing where to go. Then I remembered, I got my phone back from the cops. I tried to turn it on but it was dead. Fuck! I thought to myself. What am I going to do? I guess I got to walk home.

I was walking in circles, thinking about what could I do, until my sister's car pulled up. My love came and saved me once again. I got in the car and my sister's boyfriend was driving, with my sister in the passenger seat. I was happy to see them, man.

"Hey, bro. You okay?" "Yeah, I'm fine."

"What happened at school?"

"This kid punched me so I beat his ass."

"Jamari, you know this ain't the place for a young black man. Now you got these country folk looking to kill you. They only want to see you in two places; the graveyard or in a prison somewhere. They don't care if he hit you first. You're not supposed to fight back. Now you got a criminal case hanging over your head. You beat the hell out of that boy. The whole town is ready to riot because of you."

"Well, the judge said they're going to throw out the case because I'm a juvenile and because a fight is normal for teenage boys."

"That does not matter. People are protesting. The whole state of North Dakota is ready to get at you. Wake up! When are you going to wake up?"

I closed my mouth and didn't say another word. I wasn't going to go back and forth with Jamesha. There was no winning with her. I'll just be content I'm not in jail no more.

When we got almost 3 blocks from home, I saw police everywhere. Cars and people were all over the place, protesting my freedom. The road got more cluttered with every inch closer we got to the house. Police set up barricades and roadblocks to prevent people from stopping traffic. The ironic thing is, all these people are protesting to have me jailed but if I was murdered today, nobody would say a damn thing. I wouldn't even make the front page of the local newspaper.

A light bulb turned on in my head and I put my phone in charge. I was worried that the crowd would discover I was in this vehicle and shoot at us. I see death around the corner, like Tupac said. I'm wondering if I'm taking my last few breaths. I'm wondering if the last few images I see will be people protesting my freedom. I'm wondering if I will be assassinated and die a death similar to Malcolm X and Martin Luther King. I'm wondering if I will be immortalized for being a victim of the heated racial climate of America.

The road I'm headed down is bumpier than a teen going through puberty. I'm in the back of my sister's blue Impala, feeling like the President of Baghdad, scared of the people I hope to uplift. Only God knows what a person in that crowd has in their possession. Somebody in that crowd has my death on their Christmas list. Somebody in that crowd just wants to say that they saw me get killed.

Boop! My phone turned on and I grabbed it. The phone started vibrating from missed calls and text messages. None of that mattered right now, though. My plan is to film this hatred and let the world know what's really going on. I click on the camera app on my phone and started recording the crowd of people protesting, shouting, and hollering. I faced the camera and said, "This is what America really looks like. All of these people are gathered here today to protest my freedom. I have just been released from Williston County Jail on pre- trial release because I got into a fight with a kid at school. The kid attacked me; I was only defending myself. I don't even know the guy's name. Still no matter what the circumstance, I wish all of these people well. I want all the fine people in America to know that racism is still alive and thriving in Williston, North Dakota."

I faced the camera towards the window so the phone can capture all the people protesting and the police working hard to contain them. I turned off the camera after 2 minutes of filming.

It took us 5 minutes to get to the back of the apartment. The crazy thing was, all these people know where I lived and I didn't know Williston had this many people living in it. The police had most of the apartment blocked off, so when we arrived, they stopped us and then they noticed I was in the back seat.

The cop said, "Lay down in the back there. If these people see you, they will go crazy." I did as he said.

We finally stopped at the back, and then I started recording again but I kept the phone in my pocket. My sister opened the door and got out, then her husband. I stayed in the car, waited like 5 minutes, then I got up, opened the door, and took off running.

I was shocked to see these many people, these many cops, and these many signs. When I got out, people were already shouting but once they saw me, they went off. I saw people smoking cigarettes, others holding signs, and the rest were just being loud. The crowd was so loud I became deaf. I blocked them out. My ears were ringing.

I took off running when I heard gunshots. Bow! Bow! Bow! I started ducking while running, hoping I don't get hit. I made it to the apartment building, I ran up the stairs. On the last step, I slipped and fell down a few steps. I got up and ran back up but with more caution for my safety this time.

When I made it to the door, it was already open. I walked in and locked the door. My family was looking at me like I was the devil when I entered. Javon and Marvin were crying because of the gunshots. Jamesha was tripping and her boyfriend was bitching me out. I didn't plan for this to happen, man, WTF. They snapping on me like I planned this shit.

I went to my room, got some clothes and took a shower to wash all of the prison germs off of me. I threw away all the clothes I had on me because it was bad luck to wear clothes you went to jail in.

The house had a bad vibe in the air. The place felt foggy, like something unexpected was going to happen. Whatever it was, I was anticipating it. I walked into my room, looked out the window, and all I could see is red and blue lights.

I grabbed my phone again and decided to film another scene for the movie of my life. I recorded the video of the police lights in the darkness.

I uploaded all of the videos on my social media accounts and captioned it with a statement, saying, "Make America great again, but it never was great." I checked my page a few times, but nothing happened.

I sat my phone down and took some time out to think. The state of North Dakota is on edge because of me. I almost lost my life today. I woke up this morning in a prison cell. Damn. The police are outside to protect me from an unknown enemy. My sister has been pushed to the limit with me. She's ready to quit on me. Shit looks really shaky right now for me.

Chapter 15

I was thinking so much I fell asleep thinking about all the madness that happened in the last days. Two hours later, I hear a really loud noise coming from the living room. I hear screaming and the kids crying. Next thing I know, my door had been kicked down and a flashlight was in my face. Apparently, the FBI was raiding my house. A big AR-15 assault rifle was in my face. The police destroyed my entire home. Once I was handcuffed, they beat the crap out of me and searched my home for drugs and guns. They found nothing in the house; I was still going to jail.

In the back of my mind, I could hear terrifying screams coming from my sister as the police manhandled me throughout the whole ordeal. I wasn't really scared because I knew they didn't have a reason to arrest me. That confidence I had changed when the cop put his .38 Special to my head and pulled back the hammer. I freaked out, then the revolver went off! Bang!

Then I woke up in the middle of the night, sweating. I looked around and saw nothing. Just darkness. I figured this was it. I must take action. Something had to be done.

I went to the restroom and released all the pressure I had, then looked in the mirror. I stared at my long, beautiful, thick, dark dreadlocks and decided it was time for a change. I took a razor and cut all 63 dreads out of my head. I figured that was the reason people saw me as some type of gangster or something. The bathroom sink was full of hair. I left all of my hair in the sink and didn't bother to care about getting rid of it, my mind was made up. These people are trying to kill me and I won't let them do it that easy. I made a hasty choice to pack up all my stuff and hit the road. I put 2 pairs of everything in my backpack, grabbed my phone, and left my room.

When I made it to the living room, I started having doubts as to whether I should go or not. I started feeling desperate to do something or just stop.

I motioned to my pocket and felt a piece of paper. The paper had Abu Swiswi's wife's number on it. Perfect, I thought to myself. I went to my room and dialed the number. The phone rang a few times then went to voice mail. Shit! What the fuck I'm going to do now? I called again. It rang two times, then someone answered in a sleepy voice. "Hello, who is this?"

"This Jamari. A friend of Abu. He said to call you for some protection." "That's right. He told me all about you. I'm corning right now. Where are you?"

My face lit up when she said that. I was also kind of aroused by how sexy she sounded.

"I'm at the Kum and Go gas station by Reclamation." "I'll be there in 5 minutes."

"Okay." I didn't get a reply after that, she hung up the phone. I quickly became anxious and ran out of the house like a little school girl going out on her first date. As soon as I walked out the door, I remembered that I have to stay on high alert. People wanted to have me dead. I crept down the stairs, hoping not to make any noise while doing so.

I got outside and the area was clear. Not one person in sight. I put my hoodie on, which this time had more space due to my new hairstyle.

I started walking at a fast pace, hoping not to be detected. On my way to the gas station, I looked back and side to side with every step. Hoping to see my killer before he saw me. I felt like I was the main character of a scary movie. The world was against me but no matter how gruesome things may get, I knew deep down I was going to decide the world's fate. I was going to control my fate and run my own kingdom. I was going to be the king I was born to be.

A cool breeze passed by and the wind started whistling off the trees into my ears. A cold chill hugged my spine and my body fought to shake it off. Fuck! I said to myself in the lonely, cold streets. Then I saw a little black cat strolling down the street casually. WTF! The sight of the furry animal made me think of my dream. I got kind of scared and I started running down the street to the gas station. The cat saw me and took off but I didn't chase it, I had my own path to go down.

After a few minutes of running, my chest felt like it was going to explode, so I stopped. I'm breathing hard walking down the icy sidewalk. Looking to my left and right, I see homes with trucks and cars out front. Only a few of the homes had light coming from a window or something. Most of the homes were lights out. Only if these people knew North Dakota's most wanted was outside their home right now. What would they do?

As I was walking, still trying to catch my breath, I approached a light on the street corner. I looked down at my feet and noticed something black behind me. I got worried for a quick second, then I realized it was my shadow. "My shadow, everywhere I go, my highs and lows. My shadow, a reflection of me, without light you wouldn't see. My shadow, the dark reflection of me. Wondering with every pass will this day be my last; before I become a memory, immortalized by a repeating of history, or will I become a casualty. Born to die a victim of war, or will I have a vision like those that came before me, and foresee a victory in a battle that is bigger than you and me."

I was in deep thought when my phone vibrated and I snapped back into reality. I already knew who was calling me; Mr. Swiswi's wife. When I grabbed my phone to answer, the call dropped. Hmm, that was weird, I told myself before I dialed the number to call back. Before I could touch the call button, I got another call. I answered this one quickly. "Hello," I said.

"I'm here, where are you?" "I'm one block away."

"Alright, I'm coming to you. Stay put."

"I'm going to be on the corner by 3rd Avenue, under the street light. I'm the only person out here."

Click. The line went dead again. Shit. What to expect now? I'm suspicious at this point. I don't even know this lady or her husband. What if this was a trap? I had nothing to lose anyway. My time is coming soon. I rather die at night in the dark than in the public's eye.

Vroom! All I could see was headlights from a big truck coming my way after it hit the corner rapidly. From what I observed all my life growing up in Miami, when you see a car speeding at night, you can only do two things. Run or shoot first. Since I did not have access to a pistol, I ran for dear life. While I was running, the car turned off its lights. I looked back and the car slowed down. I started running faster. My back felt like it had holes burning in it already. I already could envision my sad story on the news; Teen fatally shot in Williston, North Dakota. No suspects have been named at this time. Call 1-800- tips to give us a tip on this boy's murder. After that night, I won't even be a story anymore. I will just become a faded memory.

My phone started vibrating on this high-speed pursuit I was on, then I realized that the big suspicious car behind me was actually a friend, not an enemy. I did not run too far anyways, these boots were holding me back, along with this big stuffed backpack. I stopped running and answered the phone. "Hello," I said while gasping for breath.

"Why are you running?"

"I thought you were someone else." "Get in the car."

I turned around and the car caught up with me. I looked at the big, all-black Chevy with the 4x4 wheels. Now that's tough, I thought to myself. I went to the passenger door and the window dropped down. All I could see was a light-skinned lady with long dark hair looking at me.

"Jamari, get in the car."

"Okay." I entered the car with very little resistance.

The car had a dreamcatcher dangling from the rearview mirror. That was the first thing to catch my eye. The second thing that caught me was how pretty Mrs. Swiswi is. She had to be about 51 but still, she was able to compete with the young bucks and still come out on top. The car is so warm and comfortable, I feel so relaxed. Mrs. Swiswi asked me, "Are you ready?"

"I guess so.," I said, unsure if I really prepared for the road ahead of me.

I fell asleep during the car ride to wherever Mrs. Swiswi took me. All I know is when I woke up, I was in a room by myself. I touched my eyes and I felt small blocks of crust in the corner of my eyes. I wiped the crumbs off my eyes and a feeling of discomfort took over me. The feeling of not being home and not being able to do what I please. This was a sacrifice I have to make to survive for now.

Looking around this room, I saw a few abnormal things. A large dreamcatcher hanging over the bed set, and a goat head with horns. I would normally freak out at the sight of these things but I'm just content to have a place to stay in peace. Oh shit, what the fuck happened to my hair? hahaha, oh yea, I chopped it off. I got scared for a second. It doesn't matter. Long hair or short hair, I'm still a black man in the white man's world.

So many emotions running through my body and it is just adding to my uneasiness. These sheets I'm lying in are extremely comfortable. Well, it's not a sheet, it's a quilt. The same kind they talked about in class growing up during black history month. Quilts are all sewed by hand and have meanings to them. They all tell stories about the creator and their family. No two quilts are the same. The slaves made them with the very limited material they had. These quilts are a rich part of African American history.

I also noticed that in this room, it had a bunch of antique items. This room has an energy I can't quite put my name on it.

Mrs. Swiswi walked in the room just like room service at a bed and breakfast hotel, holding a tray with eggs, pancakes, and sausage links. "You awake?"

"Yeah," I said eagerly.

"Why don't you eat up and get in the shower when you're done." "Sure, and thank you very, very much, Ma'am."

"No problem. We have a long day ahead of us."

I didn't reply. I was trying to figure out what she meant by a long day ahead of us. My curiosity did not last long because the smell of the food took over the room. My stomach growled as I watched the beautiful lady walk out of the room. Her hair is so long that on her way out the door, it almost caught in between the door and the wall. Luckily for her, she barely got away.

My mood changed very quickly; I was happy now. I ate breakfast in almost 5 minutes. I would have finished faster but it was hot. I even drank all of the syrup like a big kid. I placed the tray on the floor next to my backpack. I reached for my bag and pulled out a towel and an outfit. Now the only problem is, I don't know where the restroom is. I have to take a leak and shower.

Once I got the courage to walk out of the room, the home was very decorated, unlike Laurie's ghost-like home. The Indian thing was very noticeable. I walked up the hallway and I saw two doors, one on the left, one on the right. I chose to knock on the door on the left. I knocked twice with no response. This had to be the restroom. I placed my ear on the door to double-check. I didn't want to walk in on anyone doing anything.

I heard nothing, so I turned the knob and I was wrong. This was someone's room. I closed the door immediately. By now I'm nervous, so I creep over to the door on the right and turned the know. This was a restroom, so I went in and handled my business.

I got freshened up. On my way out of the shower, a feeling of pain took over me. I felt like something was missing. I just couldn't put the mark on it.

I'm back in the room, looking at this life-size dreamcatcher. This thing was magical, man. While analyzing it, I just knew that it held some sort of importance in my life. Hopefully, I will find out just exactly what is the purpose of this thing in my life here and now.

While I was having those curious thoughts, I heard a buzzing sound coming from the bed. Oh yea, my phone. Someone was calling me. I rushed to the bed and knocked over the pillow and scrambled the sheets. Still, I could not locate the cell phone. It was somewhere around, I could hear it. I looked on the floor, still no phone. Then I checked my backpack and found it. That's when it hit me, nobody calls me; I have no friends. I don't even want to speak to anyone right now. I still picked up my phone to see what was going on. I got a missed call from Jamesha that I was not going to return. I also had a lot of notifications from my social media account. The video I uploaded in my sister's car went viral.

2 million views overnight!!! This was exciting to me. I had 2 million people's attention on me. I'm glad to know that people can see the injustice this country is trying to put me through. I now have the chance to make a statement, I now have a voice people want to hear. I also had over 100,000

followers and thousands of direct messages. People are really interested in me.

I'm scrolling down my timeline and all I can see is the backlash from the black community towards the racists in North Dakota. The only thing is, people aren't physically able to do anything for me right now. Fuck! Man, I blew this shit up even bigger now. When I realized that this is now going to be a national problem, I had mixed feelings about it. Happiness and fear at the same time. Going down my timeline, the video was shared 66.3k times. Some people are planning a counter-protest for me. Meanwhile, I'm being a pussy, hiding away from the problem I created. I'm throwing rocks while living in a glasshouse.

I heard a knock on the door and quickly hid my phone like it was contraband. Mrs. Swiswi walked in and said, "Give me your phone."

I looked at her, puzzled, but feeling guilty. "What you talking about?" "Give me the damn phone before I throw you out to those damn wolves out there." As I handed her the phone, she snatched it away. "You started something that you won't finish. Once I give you your protection, don't stop by my house or call my phone no more."

My feelings were hurt when she said that because I didn't understand where the aggression was coming from. I felt ashamed of myself but it wasn't a big deal, I guess. I did make the whole situation worse by uploading the video. Mrs. Swiswi was a nice lady but I pissed her off. Lol, I have the power to do that to people. After she got the phone, she stormed off and slammed the door.

30 minutes later, she returned with 2 buckets and some supplies. I didn't say a word because I was still afraid of her after she shouted at me. For the next 20 minutes, she walked in and out, bringing various items into the

room. I was sitting on the bed wondering what was she doing. It was strange to me but my opinion doesn't matter, this ain't my house.

I started hearing a strange noise coming from the house. It sounded weird but familiar. I knew what it was. The sound started getting closer and closer, then the doorknob turned and Mrs. Swiswi walked in with a rooster. A very big one at that. I was intrigued too as to why she had a chicken. I didn't know chickens could survive out here in the snow. Back home, my neighbors had chickens and we would steal the eggs whenever they made a nest in our yard. Those chickens used to be the most annoying things in the world. Every morning at the same time, "Cock-A-Doodle-Doo!" Even on the weekends. I hated but loved small feathery animals at the same time. They gave me something to do after school. I would chase them around and make them fly. The sad thing is, they can't fly for a long time. I remember one time I came home from school and a mother chicken was roaming around my backyard and it had its chicks with her. The yellow chicks made this small light chirping all in unison. So they were in my yard and I walked towards the door in my backyard, and the mother chicken attacked me. The feathers it had all rose up and the chicken got all puffy. I screamed at full volume and started running around, crying. I couldn't believe it. All because I was not even trying to harm the animal. I was just trying to get in my house after school.

Ever since then, I stayed far away from those things. Now it's like I don't even feel threatened by the chicken's presence. I would stomp on it if it were to try me. I mean the chicken's legs were tied up, so I guess that was why I felt that way.

Chapter 16

I was busy looking at the rooster, I almost didn't see she also had a green knife and a green Native American tribal hat.

"Okay Jamari, it's time," Mrs. Swiswi said. I stared at her, confused. She had a box of matches in her hand. She started going towards one of the buckets she placed in the room earlier and struck a match and threw it in the bucket. Whish! fire was ignited. I was shocked. I did not expect that to happen. The bucket was on fire and my heart wanted to jump out my chest.

"Sit down on the floor right here," she said as she pointed to the ground next to her. The woman knelt next to me and began a prayer. "Oh God of the ancestors, please show your face to me, for today I come humbly asking for your blessing to protect this boy." After she said that, she started shaking, laughing, and jumping up and down. "Yes, Lord. Yes, my Lord. This is him, the boy, the one you asked for, yes my Lord."

The whole time, I was sitting down, terrified because now I understand what type of protection I was getting. I thought I was going to be hiding out for as long as I can, or until the heat dies down. I didn't think I would be in the middle of a voodoo ritual.

Mrs. Swiswi got up and started chanting around the room. Slowly but surely, the energy in the room shifted. I felt like I was in another world. My body was heavier, it was as if this new dimension I'm in has more intense gravity. I could not understand what was happening to me.

Mrs. Swiswi went to get a big green leaf and wrote my name on it with a black ink pen 7 times. Then she started chanting and dancing some more. After she threw the leaf in the fire, I instantly felt an electric shock run through my body. Oh shit, I'm going to die. I have to get out of here. Sadly, my destiny was on auto-pilot. I didn't have a choice but to stay; this ceremony is a part of my fate. I have to accept everything coming to me. I will do this now or forever be 3/5 of a man. Once I told myself I will accept my fate, I was not bothered by anything. Yes, I still have fear in my heart but I have to be strong. The worst is yet to come.

Mrs. Swiswi started praying again. "Yes, Lord of those that were and those that still are, this is him, the boy." She started dancing and rolling on the ground like a puppy, then she stood up before me and said, "You will change the world. Everything you fear is an illusion. You have found love but there is a seed that threatens your life. You must choose your own fate and carve your own destiny, for you have been chosen. FIGHT! WAKE UP! Or be another..." Mrs. Swiswi said in a deep voice before she fell down. The spirit of her ancestors took over her body for a while, just to speak to me. I guess I was the chosen one; A born messiah or something. Man, I'm just a regular dude. What is all this supposed to mean?

The room is hot as hell and I'm sweating, the smoke is killing me.

Man, I'm ready for all of this to be over with.

Then the word FIGHT! rang a bell in my head. FIGHT!

Mrs. Swiswi got up slowly, after 2 minutes of lying on the floor. She hit her head pretty hard. Luckily she did not have any scars or cuts or anything. She just might have a concussion, though. "Thank you, my Lord," she chanted, then she went to get the chicken.

Suddenly, I felt a force of wind come into the room with a nice cool cold breeze. Whooosh!! The fire got put out and the room was pitch black. Next thing I know, I was being restrained by at least 6 people. Well, it felt like I was being held back by people. As much as I tried to move, I couldn't. I was helpless. I got goosebumps all over my body from the cold chill that invaded the room. All I could hear was the poor chicken chirping for dear life.

20 seconds later, silence took over the room. The only thing that could be heard in the room was my freakish screams. I was mortified. This process was taking its toll on me. Being pinned down by spirits was my limit. I couldn't take it anymore, I was going crazy. I felt like a sex slave trapped in a basement for years. My only desire is to be freed of this recurring dream.

Then I felt someone touching me all over my body, feeling on my genitals and my butt, then POP! my pants are being cut off, then goes my shirt, then RIP! there goes my boxers. I feel so vulnerable and scared. "Lord, please save me, God, please, I will do anything. God, I'm sorry. Save me, please. Lord Jesus Christ save me. Please forgive me for my sins, Father. God, I'm sorry!"

The prayers started once again but this time the room seemed like a flea market with many voices shouting at one time in different directions. Oddly, one voice stuck out the most, and it was Mrs. Swiswi's soft voice. Amid this storm, she still sounded like a beauty. By the sound of it, she was close to me.

I started to feel hopeless when it started raining. I didn't know what it was but I sensed little drops of liquid spread all over my body. The sprinkle was light, not too much, definitely enough to cover my whole body in water. , only thing is, where the hell is the water coming from? Where were these voices coming from? What the hell is holding me down like this? This isn't scientifically possible; how could this be happening?

The room was as dark as night and sounded like a zoo until Mrs. Swiswi lit up another match and the fire started up all over again. All of the sounds and the restrictions went away, but that was the least of my worries at the moment. A headless chicken was running around the room chaotically. My body was smeared in blood, chicken blood. The room went soundless once again and I was in my own universe. I closed my eyes and saw a gavel drop and a crowd of people cheering. I opened my eyes and saw Mrs. Swiswi with a knife to my neck, and that's when it hit me. All of this happened before in my dream. I had already lived this before. Honestly, it seems to me like almost all of my dreams come true. What could explain this process to me? Mrs. Swiswi cut a small piece of my neck and it started bleeding rapidly. I passed out after so much went out of me. The last few things I remember was her bathing me with some sort of leaf mixture with alcohol. All I know is every time she passed the leaves on my body, it stung. She also made me drink a portion of some sort. The elixir was nasty as hell. It made me want to vomit but I couldn't. Lastly, I remember a brown rattlesnake with very vibrant green eyes slithering around the room. I was too weak at this point to pay any real attention to it. I was on my way to being unconscious.

Throughout the whole process, I was in constant fear. Physics and science didn't have anything on that. I mean, I'm Haitian and my family back home does similar   rituals and festivals   but   I didn't expect anything like   that.   My grandmother was the one that was deep in that stuff but she passed away before I was born, so I never got to see that side of my culture. I always knew that stuff existed, but the first-hand experience is different. I sure I am a believer now. I always thought that stuff was hogwash. The only thing is if people are able to channel energy and call on spirits and ancestors to do all of this powerful magic, why isn't the whole world doing it? Why does society put such a negative view on voodoo and other similar religions? Granted, the process was a little bit scary but that type of power could be tapped into for good to benefit the world. The white folks want to hide our power from us at the end of the day. They want to keep the sacred knowledge of those that came before us for themselves. They are trying to trick us into thinking that this stuff is wrong when the

Pope at the Vatican is doing the same thing. They try to make blacks and people of color look like boogie men.

I woke completely naked and shaking from the cold air in the room. I turned my head 90 degrees left then 180 degrees right. There was not one sign or trace of what happened yesterday. No blood, no leaves, no smoke, no ashes. Nothing. Mrs. Swiswi must have done one hell of a job cleaning up the place. The real question is, where the hell are my clothes? Because I'm not going to stay butt naked all day.

As I searched for clothes to put on my body, a grenade went off in my stomach. Boom! I was hungry as hell and I felt weaker than Superman when he's around kryptonite.

I got up and saw a set of clothes on the bed, laid out perfectly, like how my mom used to do it before I go to school. I quickly put on all my clothes, hoping someone doesn't see my nakedness. After I put my clothes on, I sat around waiting for something to happen. When nothing happened, I decided to leave the room. I clutched on the doorknob but it wouldn't budge. Hmm... too weak and tired to get worked up over the locked door, so I went to bed. I already went through the valley of death, being alive was good enough for me.

Mrs. Swiswi walked into the room while I was lying down and dropped off some food. I was acting like I was asleep but I wasn't. She dropped by just to check on me, I guess. The food smelled good. I don't know why I acted like I was asleep. I didn't want to do any more of those crazy rituals. The first one already took all my energy. The second one is going to kill me.

As soon as she left, I smashed the food. Now I had nothing to do and by then I was already tired of being in that room. I walked right out the door, and to my surprise,   the door wasn't locked. I went towards the living room, fascinated by all the Native American art. Those were some beautiful paintings. Native American culture is amazing. The Native Americans or Indians as they call them, are the original people of the land I live in. Sadly, they were also slaughtered to build this country. Screams, blood, and flesh of the Native Americans made the land of the free. Meanwhile, the original inhabitants are being pushed to live on reservations. They stole the land from these people. While I'm gazing at the scenery in the living room, I sensed a tingling sensation in my hands. I wanted to touch all of this fine stuff, but I knew better than that.

Mrs. Swiswi crept up behind me while I was checking out all this and scared the fuck out of me. "What are you scared for? The gods are with you." "Ahh..." I said, looking intimidated.

"Come on, let's sit down so I can explain to you everything." She led me to her vintage couch and we both took a seat, then she started to speak. "You see, my husband had a dream he would meet a boy that possessed a special power while he was in prison. He did not really make much of the dream but when he told me about it, I told him to pray to the gods of our ancestors about it and when he did, they told him the boy will change the world but only with his assistance. So when you came around and he saw your situation, he knew that it was you.•. That's why I took you in. Now, the ceremony that you did was for protection against all things, from spiritual to the physical world. Anything that tries to oppose you will face the wrath of the gods. I also did a reading for you and your future has a lot in store. You will have to overcome this first. Now, the ancestors also said that the hole in your heart will be filled with joy, with true love, a bond that will be indestructible but on the other hand, there is something or someone., that might jeopardize that."

"Wow," I muttered under my breath, I'm still in disbelief that I am going through this. I'm also hopeful, too, that I will find true love. "What am I supposed to do? Me... change the world? Mrs. Swiswi, what power do I possess? Because I mess up everything I touch. If that's what you call a special power, then I'm very talented."

"I don't know what power you have. It's up to you to build your connection with the ancestors and that's what we started during your ceremony." "This is a lot for me to take in. I just don't want to die. I'm not ready to go yet."

"You will be fine, I assure you, son. You did a 3-day ceremony. You slept for 3 days and during that time frame, your spirit was in front of the gods' pedestal. You were rid of all of those bad spirits that followed you for so long and you were bathed for good luck so that you will have favor wherever you go."

"What! I slept for 3 days! How is that possible? My sister is probably going crazy!"

"Jamari, don't worry. Your sister called your phone and I said you were fine and I'm hiding you," she said you should call her if you need anything

"What about the people? Are they still protesting?"

"Well, it's been snowing really hard, so no one in North Dakota is protesting but the rest of the country is flared up. The video you put out went viral and people are really riding for you in Miami, Chicago, L.A., New York, Atlanta, Houston, and many other cities. They have been protesting for the past

3 days; so far, nothing outrageous has occurred. Jamari, this is really serious.

Lives are on the line and so is yours as well. You must make the right decision." I felt like I got struck by lightning when those words left her mouth. I'm in the eye of a category 5 hurricane and my house is built on an unstable foundation. Plenty of rain is getting on my head and my thoughts are being flooded with doubt. I can't evacuate from the mind of a maniac. The damage from this storm will be unrepairable. "What do you suppose I do, Mrs. Swiswi?"

"I suggest you stay here and pray to the gods yourself." "How can I do that?"

"The same way everyone else does."

"Mrs. Swiswi, you know when you did the ceremony, it felt like deja vu. I had a dream all of this happened before. The circumstance was different but the main thing was the same."

"That is the hoe, the ancestors speak to you, through your dreams. You have a gift. Pay attention to your dreams and manifest them to be what you want." Somehow my life has turned out to be a twisted fantasy. Only God knows what's next for me. I stared at Mrs. Swiswi with a serious face but I didn't respond. The cat had my tongue, I guess.

Chapter 17

Mrs. Swiswi had got a text on her phone. I guess it was from her kid. She left in a rush and said she had to go pick up her children from school. I found that kind of odd, how she had a child. This house did not seem like a place for a little kid. I now sat in the living room by myself, lonely. There was no TV in here. The centerpiece of the room is a stuffed bear with a life-size dream catcher on the opposite side. Feathers on a Chief crown stood on top of a bookcase. I adore the scenery, the culture of the natives is something I have to get into. Maybe I'll ask Mrs. Swiswi what all this stuff means when she gets back. I looked at the dream catcher one more time and noticed that it was lighting up. I rubbed my eyes to make sure I wasn't tripping. The light went away after that; if it was really there, I don't know.

I started thinking about the whole thing and I felt exasperated. This is too much for me, man. I'm never going to make it. I might as well die right now. I'm going to get killed anyways.

Oh shit, Carmena's funeral passed already. Damn. I did not even get the chance to call her family or anything. That's such a waste man, she was so young. As these thoughts were running through my mind, I could feel my heart freeze. It stopped for 10 seconds and began beating fast to make up for the lost time. Then I heard keys at the door. Tears almost came out but since I heard a noise, I had to suck it up. I don't want no one to think I'm a little bitch.

I laid down on the couch like I was just chilling the whole 30 minutes she was gone. Mrs. Swiswi entered the home still looking like the darling she is. I waited to see her kid. I expected her to be walking hand in hand with her little one.

"Hey, Jamari." "Hi Mrs. Swiswi."

An echo filled my head. "Your heart will be filled with joy with true love." WTF! Mrs. Swiswi is too old for me and she's married. No way!

"Oh shit, this is not possible!" I said as my jaw lowered at the sight of Keylina walking into the room. She hadn't noticed me yet, her head was still down while she was stomping the snow out of her shoes. Keylina looked identical to her mother but she was more beautiful. It was clear where she got her looks from. Her hair was tied up in a ponytail with long black hair going down. She wore a burgundy jacket, a black shirt, and black jeans. Keylina possessed supernatural energy, the room lit up as soon as she stepped in. Damn, Keylina is absolutely charming. The girl is so pretty; seeing her makes me feel like a kid when they get a kiss on the cheek from their mom.

She walked into the house, closed the door behind her, then she screamed when she saw me. It was as if I was some kind of celebrity. She ran to me and jumped on me. I was smiling the whole time. A feeling of tranquility took over me. She kissed me on my lips in front of her mom. I have to admit, I was worried about her morn's reaction. But having her next to me felt so good. I know this was where I was supposed to be. I made the right decision coming here, even though my ears were on fire from feeling slightly embarrassed in front of Mrs. Swiswi.

"What are you doing here, Jamari?" "Uhh...II

"How do you know this boy, Keylina?" "He goes to my school."

"Yeah, we…"

Mrs. Swiswi looked furious but she was trying to get some clarity as to why her daughter was all over this very troubled boy. "Keylina, I'm going to ask you again. How do you know this boy?"

"Mom, he's my boyfriend. We go to the same school. The only school in the county," Keylina said with an attitude.

I was caught in the middle of a standoff, looking up at Mrs. Swiswi awkwardly.

"Since when... How long have y'all been dating?" "Well..."

"Only a few weeks. He's a very nice guy. He's not what the media is making him out to be."

"Keylina, you're too young to have a boyfriend. You're still in school." "Mom!"

"Mrs. Swiswi, I just want to say…"

"Uh uh, this does not concern you. This is a conversation between my daughter and me."

"Mom, so if I can't be with him, then why is he here?" "I did something for him."

"So he's one of your patients?"

"Yes, he needs protection. You know what's going on." "Ohh."

I stayed silent because I was ashamed of myself. Then Mrs. Swiswi walked away and went to her room. I'm guessing she is okay with us being together. Keylina kissed me again when her mom left but this time we exchanged a tongue kiss. She tasted so good. This kiss was like a transfer of energy. My manhood instantly got inflated. Keylina is looking at me so passionately. This is the type of moment that made life worth living; having a beautiful girl at your side at times like this.

"What happened, Jamari?"

"Man, it's a long story. I don't really want to speak about it right now." "Come on, you can tell me. You trust me, don't you?"

The situation did not have anything to do with trust. I really didn't want to speak about it but in order to prove to her that I do trust her, I spilled the beans. "Man, I walked out of class and I got blindsided by this kid and we started fighting. So when we got to the Principal's office, he called the cops and when I went to jail, I met this guy Abu, and that's how I got here. Well, that's the short version of it."

"You know that you're famous and all over TV and the internet. You are the talk of the nation."

"I didn't know I was that big. To be honest, Keylina, I want all of this to be over with."

"Don't worry about that right now, you'll be fine. I'm assuming that you know Laurie went missing. She wrote a letter to her family saying that she's running away."

"Wow!" I felt some sort of way but I have to worry about myself right now. She was the last thing on my mind. Besides, I got Keylina, I don't need her. "She is the reason why you're in all of this shit. Her boyfriend is Freddy Willis."

"Who's that?"

"The boy you fought. Y'all fought because he found out that you left with her during Steve Wentz's party. Steve told him that you said you fucked her in her car. Jamari, those guys are not your friends. And I didn't know you smoked weed. Honestly Jamari, you should have known all of these guys are out to get you."

Everything clicked in my head. I put all of the pieces of the puzzle together. I was a fool for thinking that these guys were my friends. "Keylina, you're right but ain't nothing I could do now."

"You got me, Jamari. You don't need anybody else."

I didn't want to say I was not expecting that. Those words warmed up my heart but I'm still unsure if I can trust right now. Honestly, my heart is an unstable place right now. So I stayed silent and gave her a kiss. We started making out and things got real heated up. The only thing was, we were still in her living room, so we just started talking about life. Keylina and I share a lot of the same ideals. We both want to get married and have children. We both want to empower our people and make a way for people in poverty. She wants to be a businesswoman and I want to be an artist. I do see myself owning a business in my future but I want to make modern art from my Haitian culture.

Keylina is just a lovely girl all around and getting to know her makes me like her even more. If I survive this, I will marry her and take care of her for the rest of my life. I will show her how much I appreciate her for making me happy and being here for me. I just hope this isn't all stripped from me and I have to do prison time.

The day passed by real fast with Keylina keeping me company. She seemed to be happier to be with me than I with her. I didn't know she liked me that much. I was in a good place for the most part, although I had so much on my mind all of that seemed minor. Keylina was my main focus right now. Damn, man... I might have to give this up. I'm going to fight.

It started getting late so Keylina and I both decided to go to bed. She insisted that I go to sleep with her but I couldn't do that. Mrs. Swiswi will throw me out of the house. I can't afford that. I gave her a big kiss and a hug and went to "my room". I got in bed thinking about how crazy my life is. This is like a weird dream. I hope I survive it all to wake up the next morning. This will all come to an end one day. Until then, I will remain strong. I can get through this. Even if I don't survive, Carmena and I will meet at the Heavenly gates. Tossing and turning in my bed, thinking about my future, and all the possible outcomes. I don't know what awaits me but I will face it like a man.

When I finally went to sleep, an hour passed.

Steel gates, barbed wire, and a watchtower. Officers watching over prisoners in the penitentiary, with fully loaded shotguns in hand. A big white wall is the only thing separating the world's greatest criminals from the free world.

1:00 pm. "The compound is open for a 10-minute move," was said over the prison P.A. system. Orange jumpsuits and guys in basketball shorts filled the yard. Whites on one side of the yard, blacks on the other, and Mexicans in the corner. A few guys shirtless, lifting weights in the sun. Small clicks of gang bangers all in their own place. Prisoners exchanging contraband for postage

stamps. Smoking, drinking, and laughing all going on the rec yard. From far away, one would assume that everyone was having fun. Every single person in the yard is carrying a knife. Very sad it will be for the man caught without his. A young black man from southern Florida just arrived on the compound. He decided to walk the track and take some stress off of his mind. He just got 50 years for first-degree murder. 20 years old, still unknown to the laws of federal prison. While walking the track, he saw a transgender woman and said, "WTF?" The transgender said nothing and went her way. The boy had never seen anything like that boy before. It was a complete shock to him. He continued to walk around the track, thinking about his 2-year-old son that was born while he was in prison. The love of his life left him to be with his best friend. Thinking about it every day pains him to death.

In his neighborhood, he was a notorious drug dealer that was known for murdering those who opposed him. Been in the street all his life. He worked hard since he was 12 years old to build his legacy. His pride is too high to let him accept the fact that his right-hand man is making love to his wife. The young man called home every day for 30 days straight and she stopped answering the phone. All he wants to do is speak to his son and let her know how much he loves her.

The world came crashing down on this boy way too fast. One day he is the man of the city and the next day he becomes a faded memory.

Two years passed by and the streets he admired so much forgot he ever stood there. By the time he is expected to leave prison, he will be at least 65 years old. Sad to say, he will not leave prison. Every day, thoughts of regret run wild in his mind. The young man killed a rival gang member for his right-hand man. Now the same man is taking his place in his family. All of these thoughts ran through his mind when he was confronted by 3 blood gang members. All of these guys were big guys, with gold and tattoos all over their bodies. "What you said to my girl, nigga!"

The young man looked at those guys confused but his fight or flight instinct went off and he punched the guy in his mouth and all of his gold teeth came out his mouth. Sadly, that was all he could do because right after that, the boy got stabbed by the gang members at least 50 times. The boy's guts was on the floor. Boom!! Sirens went off. Shots were fired from the watchtower. Everyone got on the floor. The whole building was now on lockdown while a riot started on the rec yard.

By the time all of the noise was silenced, the young man lost his life. The kid expired under a rusty knife. The prison system is a black man's trap. They build more prisons than schools nowadays.

Then I woke up out of sleep, heart beating fast and sweaty. That dream felt so real, like I knew the guy all my life. Now I'm sleepy but afraid to go to sleep. I'm also thinking about the chance of me dying the same way. What if I get sent to prison behind this case?

This stuff is like a cycle for us young black men, school, prison, or death. Those who make it out are few. It seems like all we are owed in this life is poverty and death.

"Dear God, the king of all kings, please help me. I need help. If you help me make it out of this, I promise I will never mess up again. Protect me from all those trying to harm me. Thank you, God. Amen." After my prayer, I felt some kind of relief from the pain and wrong I was feeling. A Higher Power was always a part of my mind growing up but I never really paid religion any mind. I always knew voodoo was real and that most of my Haitian friend's parents took part in it but I was not that close to it. I guess I have to do some research on my own culture.

I heard a creak at my bedroom door. I faced the door, curious, wondering what made that noise but all I could witness was the absence of any light in the room. Then I felt someone get in the bed with me. At first, I was unsure but I knew it could only be one person, Keylina. I got up while she crept under the sheets. "Hey man, what are you doing?" "I hate sleeping alone."

I grabbed her and laid down with her. I instantly got an erection just by being this close to her. Keylina's hair was touching my skin, which made a sensation run all through my body. I started feeling on her. At first, I was skeptical but trying won't hurt. She didn't fight back, move my hands, or anything. From that moment, I was all in. As I started touching, I noticed that I was feeling all of her flesh and that she was in fact naked already. All she had on was a big white shirt.

My manhood wanted to break my pants but I was still too scared to go that far. Keylina looked at me and I kissed her. We start kissing madly. I felt her up and down. Keylina got on top and we were kissing, when she reached for my pants and motioned for me to take them off. So, I started undressing as fast as I could. Once my boxers slipped off, all I felt was a very glorious and warming feeling. My manhood was inside of her. I began stroking although I was new to this, the feeling of pleasure drove me in the right direction. We were making sweet and passionate love. I was kissing her while she was riding me.

Then I felt another sensation in my penis that told me to keep going. Then I ejaculated in Keylina. I kept on going even though I came already. 2 minutes later, I stopped and laid down. I was tired and needed a break.

Keylina's sexy voice made me aroused. Just hearing her moan made me want to keep going.

Then we both laid down with each other. She wanted to cuddle and I for some reason did not want to. I still cuddled up with her but I was sort of uncomfortable. Then it dawned on me that I lost my virginity to Keylina and that feeling of sex was so good. The feeling is unlike anything else. Now it all made sense. This is the feeling that got so many people killed. This was the feeling that the kids in school were always talking about. This was the feeling that many young men hustled in the street for. This was the feeling I have been missing.

I can't believe this; I had sex with Keylina. Never could I have ever imagined this. I feel so nonchalant.

While Keylina and I were laid up cuddling, Mrs. Swiswi burst into the room. "What the fuck is going on?"

"Oh shit." My heart dropped. Keylina held onto the sheets to cover herself, while I was lying there in complete embarrassment. My cock went from rock hard to soft. I was not expecting that.

"Keylina, what are you doing? You know what? I want this boy out of here by tomorrow morning."

We both stayed in the bed silent until she left. I was mad embarrassed by this situation.

Then Keylina said when she left, "Don't worry about my mom. She's not going to do shit."

"I think it's best if you get to your room."

"We already got caught. What's the worst that could happen?" I laid there still, not knowing what to expect.

We started making love again after minutes of silence. There was nothing I could lose anyways. She already made up her mind and Keylina knows her mom better than I.

By the morning time, when I woke up, Keylina was gone. She had to go to school, while I was in her home.

I woke up reminiscing on the beautiful night Keylina and I had.

I miss her already, although she was probably gone only for a few hours.

Then Mrs. Swiswi walked into the room and I got spooked. She came in calm and explained to me that she had a dream and the spirits told her that Keylina and I were blessed by the ancestors, so she doesn't have a problem with us dating. That was a surprise to me. I thought she came to run me out of her home. Mrs. Swiswi is very gorgeous, man, looking at her makes me think of her daughter. Damn, they look just alike. Fascinated by the beauty of an older woman, old enough to be my mother.

Days passed and it was the same routine over and over. Wait for Keylina to come home and have sex with her all day. I was very happy. I was on top of the world. Spending all my days with my wonderful wife, Keylina. Things seemed like I was in a fantasy world living a happy ever after but that was far from the truth.

Chapter 18

Sitting in a room, trying to devise a plan to come out on top, while feeling that my destiny was already made out for me but still I'm trying to change it. Waiting for my love to come home. She's at school for now and I'm just waiting in her room, watching TV That's all I have done for the past few days; eat, sleep, pray, and have sex. These days have been really nice because of Keylina and her mother. I owe them the world, and I promise I will pay them back. Mrs. Swiswi walked into the room and said, "Son, here's the phone. It's your sister calling."

I answered the phone questioning why she called but nonetheless, I was thrilled she called. "Hello."

"Hello."

"Jamesha, what's up?" "Hey, bro. How are you?"

"I'm doing fine. What about you?"

"Good. Your attorney called and said you have a court date today but you don't have to show up for the arraignment because he will plead not guilty for you."

"Attorney? What are you talking about? You got me a lawyer?"

"Well, the guy said he wants to be your attorney because he understands this is a high profile case and he doesn't want you misrepresented. He's with Black Lives Matter."

My face lit up with a big smile. Now I had a fighting chance. "Okay, sis. Thank you very much. I love you!"

"I love you too, bro. Call me if you need anything."

"For sure, sis. Bye. I love you." Click. Damn, I had a court appearance today and I didn't even know.

Mrs. Swiswi gave me her hand, implying that I give her the phone back. Then she said, "What did she say?"

"I had a court date but my lawyer went for me. I didn't have to go."

"Had I known, I would have done something for you but I'm sure you will be fine."

"Yes, ma'am, I sure hope so."

Then she exited the room. I shook my head in disappointment. Things were out of my hands.

In order to get my mind off the news, I grabbed the remote and started channel surfing. Nothing was really ever on TV nowadays anyways. As I skipped through the channels, I saw reality shows, cartoons, and sports TV; the same old stuff. Then I passed the local news channel and the headline read Breaking News: Jamari Picard goes to court for arraignment.

My eyes grew really wide and my heart started speeding like a Lamborghini. Live from the scene, the reporter was in a background filled with hundreds of protestors and Trump supporters. Some had signs and others were shouting, "Make America great again, make black people slaves again." On National TV this bigotry was being broadcasted. Police were everywhere. They set up a barricade to stop people from messing with people entering the courthouse. I was amazed at how far this had gotten. There were reporters and cameramen flashing photos. They were waiting for my arrival but luckily I didn't have to show up today. I don't think I would have reacted too well to all of that.

Now I have to mentally prepare myself for all of this because there is a chance I might have to step in that courthouse. The headline changed, "Picard pleads not guilty. Did not appear in court. The attorney appeared in his presence." My heart sank even further from where it already was. My attorney walked out of the courthouse and he was rushed by people, journalists, and cameramen. My attorney, a black man, put himself in the line of fire for me, a kid he doesn't even know or hasn't met. My case for him was a chance to do a self-serving act of kindness, I doubt he even cares about me. He just wants to be known as the lawyer that goes down in the books as the one that beat that high profile case. Still, I had some respect for him because he was being filmed on TV being almost eaten alive by the media personnel. They asked him for a statement but he refused to speak. I was hoping for a speech. One that would be forever marked in the history books but I wasn't getting that.

I looked at the TV like my life depended on it. My lawyer kept his head down and avoided the cameras as much as possible until his ride showed up and pulled off. Very dangerous position to be in, man. And yet, I was the cause of all of this drama. That's when the reality of my circumstances actually sunk into my skin. My case will form history as we know it. The outcome of this case may change the world as we see it.

I turned the TV off and the images from the screen contaminated my head. I felt like I was right there. I could hear all of the voices shouting and screaming in my ear. "Make America great again, make black people slaves again" was echoing in my brain. I could sense the pure hatred in their faces. These are the people that made our President get elected. These are the white supremacists that normally hide in the shadows. These are the kind of people that are in public offices. These are the people that represent America's three colors. The veil of hatred is too thick, covering their eyes, leaving them forever blind to their ignorance. So much malice for a young man their eyes have never met. You would have thought they were the people that were held captive and tortured for 300 years. You would have thought they were the people that had to sit in the back of the bus. You would have thought they were the people being profiled and killed by the police. You would have thought they were the ones living in crime and drug-infested neighborhoods. This doesn't make sense. How sick could these people be? Blacks are not the problem, we are the solution. "Break us down, build us up. No longer are we giving in, we must overcome the condition we living in. Wherever there is light, there is life. A darker night makes for a brighter day." Dreams are dreams and I'm forced to live in reality. Wishing I could sleep my day away so I can live in an alternate reality because this life is not for me. Hoping I can rise to higher grounds.

Keylina came home and I was asleep on her bed. She woke me up and I smiled when I saw her lovely face. "Wassup baby," I said with a groggy voice.

"You saw the news. Everyone was talking about your court date at school!" "Yeah, I saw it. My sister called this morning."

"When is your next court date?"

"I don't know, actually. I'm going to call my sister and find out." "Okay."

"How was your day, beautiful?"

"My day was good. You have been on my mind all day."

I grabbed Keylina and we started wrestling. She tried to fight back but she couldn't. The play fighting led to us kissing and all of our clothes ended up on the floor. The lovemaking started and ended just as quickly. One round and that was it for me today. I didn't want to keep going. This court stuff was stressing me out. It's like nobody can understand me, man. Keylina, that's my baby but she doesn't know how I feel. No matter how much I explain to her, she will not understand. It's as if I'm falling in a never-ending quicksand. No matter how much I slip and fall, it's like I can't get up.

I picked up the remote and decided to look at the news some more, only to be even more shocked. Black dominated cities all over the country were all standing up and rallying for me. They all were protesting. They chanted, "Guilty of being black." Chicago, Miami, Missouri, L.A., and many other cities were all over the national news. Police squads were trying their best to contain the crowds of thousands of people. This was a beautiful sight to see, man. All of these people working together to accomplish the same goal; helping me not go to prison.

The news headline read, "Breaking News: Protest breaks out all over the country." The news reporter said, "It seems that Jamari Picard has gathered quite a following after his videos went viral after being protested and shot at by protestors in North Dakota. President Donald Trump has spoken out on it as well. He says this may be a state of emergency if all of this continues. I was dumbfounded. Even the President of the United States knew who I was.

I'm close to being a threat to national security. Just when my interest in saying something rose. I knew in the back of my head that now was not the time to speak because I might spark a flame I can't tame.

"Jamari, the next time you go to court you will have to deal with a crowd that big outside of the courthouse. And you got the President talking about you."

"Fuck the President. He's a racist piece of shit. When cops are killing all of these black kids every day, he doesn't say that is a state of emergency." Anger started to fill my mind. The POTUS not only has something negative to say but the man also is never positive. He will put black people down by any means necessary.

Chapter 19

3 months ago I was afraid of this day. Now I can't wait to get this over with. I go to court in 5 hours, man. This is the biggest day of my life. The judge assured me that this case would be dropped. 100 days later, I'm due in court for trial. I met with my lawyer one time, explained to him what happened that day and he told me that I'm going to beat this case.

I'm scared, man. I can't sleep. People all over the country have been anticipating this day. I'm facing up to 5 years max for this, man. I'm praying I come out on top. The spirits are on my side, I should be fine. Over these past few months, I've grown a lot. I came to value life a lot more. I understand why love is so important. I also have become a beacon of light that will shine over racial injustice all over the country. I'm an icon, although I have been relatively a ghost on social media and I have not provided the flame with more gas. I'm still the fire behind all of the smoke. With the help of the Most High and the ancestors, I will prevail.

The past few days have put a lot of stress on me and I have wrongly taken it out on Keylina. We had a big fight 3 days ago and she been mad ever since. We still sleep together and have sex but she been having weird attitudes lately. I know she wishes the best for me, so I ain't sweating it.

I love that girl with all my heart and after this case is done with, I will ask for her hand in marriage. Keylina is worth it, man. All of the pain and the stress. If I have to do some time, at least I had the moment to spend time with her. A life-changing experience, man. I'm thankful for all of it.

Lying in bed with the most beautiful girl in the world by my side. Nothing can beat this feeling. Thank God for Keylina.

My bladder is full and I don't want to get up. Looking at Keylina is the most tranquil sensation. I got up slowly, hoping not to wake the sleeping beauty. I crept out of the bed and entered the restroom. I turned on the light and it burned my sleepy eyes. Fuck! I blinked a few times and lifted the toilet seat. I began to urinate and I sensed a little pressure leave my stomach. When I flushed, I noticed I was a little inaccurate and left piss on the rim of the toilet. I grabbed some tissue, cleaned it up, and dropped the tissue in the basket.

That's when something caught my eye. A white stick was in there. I got curious and picked it up out of the trash. It was a pregnancy test, and it read one line for negative and two lines for positive. The small test screen had two lines.

My stomach began rumbling. The piss turned into diarrhea that quick. Within a split second, I was sicker than an orphan on Christmas Day. Is she really pregnant? Why didn't she tell me? We can't keep the baby. How long has she been pregnant?

Damn, I gotta go to court in a little while. What am I supposed to do? I can't make them take care of the baby while I'm in prison. If she has the baby, then she won't forget me if I go to prison. Plus I might have a little me walking around.

I'm in no position to make a child, man. I can't take care of the baby. Well, there is a strong chance I might die, so having an offspring isn't that bad. At least my blood will live on. Wonder if it's a boy or a girl. I have to wake Keylina up. I have to get a confirmation on this.

The irony of it all was, I walked in the restroom hoping not to wake the queen but now I left the restroom with all intent to wake her up. I approached the bed and saw her sleeping. A rapid thought of remorse ran in my mind but ran out just as fast. I had to get an answer NOW!

So, I grabbed all the sheets, threw them on the floor, and shook Keylina as fast but as gentle as possible. She felt so fragile in her sleep. She also looked so innocent. There was no way this girl could be carrying a baby.

She rose up with a shocked gasp, her eyes opened so wide.

"Keylina, baby, what's this?" I said with the pregnancy test in my hand. "Huh, what are you talking about?" she responded with a half-sleep voice.

I was not going to get anywhere like this, so I left her for 20 seconds to go turn on the lights. Once the lights were on, I went and woke her up again. This time, she was paralyzed by the light like a vampire holding her eyes. "What do you want, Jamari?"

"What is this? Are you pregnant?"

"Oh my God!" she said, holding her head. "Why didn't you tell me?

Keylina started sobbing while her hands were on her face. That's when I understood that I went about this all wrong. I went to Keylina, to caress her and show her some affection but she tried to fight me off of her. I had to eat 2 suckers to the face but I did not let go. I wanted her to know that I'm here.

"Baby, I'm sorry. I wanted you to know after you came home from court. You already have enough on your mind."

"I know princess, it's going to be alright," I said, then I gave her a soft kiss on her head. I was holding her to comfort her but tears were starting to roll down her eyes slowly. Although she couldn't see, I knew she could feel my energy. I assured her that we will be fine. I also advised her to get some sleep for both her and my child. I tucked her and Jamari Jr. back to sleep.

I stayed up thinking about what do I do? Then I figured I should shower and get ready for my big day. When I was finished getting prepared, I walked to the living room and took a seat on the couch by the life-size dreamcatcher. I sat in the fairly lit room and stared at the wall.

The next thing I remember is Mrs. Swiswi tapping me on the head to get up. I leaped up because I thought I was late. I was not late, but Mrs. Swiswi had to do a ritual for me before I left for court. I don't know what the exact time was but I knew that I didn't have much longer.

I followed Mrs. Swiswi into her special prayer room. There were feathers all over the walls and pictures of Indians on the walls and candles lit under every photo. I have been in this house for months now and I never saw this room before. It turns out that this wasn't just an ordinary closet. This also had a door connecting to Mrs. Swiswi's room as well. I look around amazed by the culture in the room. There were spears, arrows, chief hats with feathers, and plenty of other things. What stuck was the small tree she had growing in the back.

I got on my knees in front of one of the photos as she commanded me to. Mrs. Swiswi led the prayer but this time it was in her native tongue because I did not understand a word. I closed my eyes and said, "Lord, please protect me from all evil and please follow me into the courthouse so I can beat this case and be with Keylina for the rest of my life. Please Lord of all Lords... Thank you. Amen." I ended the prayer but kept my eyes closed. Then I felt something tapping me on the shoulders. It was Mrs. Swiswi. She gave me a potion to drink, so I chugged it. I gagged on it and almost threw up. It was terrible; it tasted like sewer water. Then she held my head and said a prayer. After that, she handed me a green leaf that was dipped in some perfume. That thing smelled wonderful. She instructed me to place the leaf in my shoe, and every time I stepped on the shoe in court, the judge or the attorney would choke on their words and stay silent. Then she rubbed the colon on my body and put a cross on my head 7 times with the colon. Then she told me to stand up.

That was it, I guess. This time it was nothing extreme like the first time. I was happy about that. Then Mrs. Swiswi walked to the small plant in the corner and picked a leaf or something, I guess. When she returned she said, "This is God's plant. This will take care of all the stress and anxiety you will feel." She grabbed the long Indian chief pipe under the biggest shrine and said, "This is for you." I look confused while I packed the pipe and lit up the fire. The amazing thing was, she was letting me use all of these special things from my ancestors. I didn't know what to do until she told me when to inhale from it, and so I inhaled. The smoke combated my lungs and my chest but I did not cough or exhale. Mrs. Swiswi started chanting, then I was told to exhale after like 2 minutes. I blew the smoke out with ease.

Mrs. Swiswi looked at me and said, "You did it like a true Sioux Chief." Then she laughed and said, "The potion was mushroom rum and the leaf was weed. That's what the ancestors used when they needed to reach the gods."

I didn't know if I was to laugh and play it off or if I should be mad. But I did feel a lot better.

I waited in the living room while the ladies were getting dressed. They took forever but you know that's how the ladies do.

I had an hour and 30 minutes until showtime. The clock seemed to be ticking real fast. Hopefully, the sand in my hourglass doesn't run out today. I don't think the creator would be very pleased to meet me today. 17 years old with a baby on the way and I'm facing a possible prison sentence.

On the way to the courthouse, I was in total despair. The outcome of this trial would change my life forever. The car felt like an igloo. Although we were so close to each other, I felt so isolated, like I was on a tiny boat, drifting in the sea. The only known thing that could be heard was the motor of the vehicle. Keylina tried talking to me once but I ignored her. I was lost in the jungle of my thoughts.

Until I heard the sirens of squad cars rush past our car. WTF? I looked up at the window and I saw police cars everywhere. The red and blue lights on the white on blue cars shook my heart. They also woke me up. The snowy white and grey concrete was the only thing that made me calm.
I tried my best to keep my focus on that but the police cars kept flying by.

As we got nearer to the courthouse, the more cop cars, and regular cars we saw. The traffic started clogging up real fast. There were plenty of people walking around like they were tourists on South Beach.

By then it was 30 minutes until showtime. The stuff Mrs. Swiswi gave me did not work for anything. I was still nervous as hell. At least I still had my secret weapon, and knowing I had that power provided me with some closure for now. I could possibly cripple the judge if I wanted.

Suddenly I heard a mass chopping above the car. Then I glared at the front windshield as the noise went away, I noticed a helicopter in the sky. The chopper had a news station logo that stated Channel 3 News.

When we arrived at the courthouse, the streets were blocked off by cops. People were restrained by barricades placed by the city officials. Judging from the number of cops around, the city had to make a special contract for today because there were at least 500 officers outside. Everything was under control. Yeah, things seemed chaotic but my real battle was in the courtroom. I will deal with the 10,000 rednecks another time.

I was also exhilarated when I saw at least 5,000 blacks standing in the cold to support me. That was an encouraging sight to see. The whole scene outside of the courthouse looked like a yin and yang sign. Blacks on the left, whites on the right. There were also a few whites and Hispanics on the left side. I was also glad to know that all whites weren't ignorant. There are a few good white folks on the earth. Staring outside of the dark tint, looking at the crowd of people packed in the snow like sardines, I was ready to open the door and step out the car,. when I realized this might be my last time being this close to Keylina again, so I said, Keylina. And when she turned to me, I gave her a nice kiss on her sweet lips.

At the end of the kiss, Keylina said, I love you, bae.
I love you too, princess. Then I took a deep breath and stared at the brick and mortar walls one more time. All of the people and the news reporters with cameras startled me but I had to fight.

I opened the car door and all I could hear was noise. People shouting, police walkie talkies, and reporters rushing me to ask questions. A thin wisp of cold air tapped my nose. I smelled death around the corner. Hopefully, I don't die as an outlaw.

I put my head down and tried my best to block my face from the hundreds of cameras. The crowd started screaming like I was a celebrity coming on stage for a magical performance. People were reaching out to touch me, cell phones were out and everything. There was a chopper in the sky, broadcasting the overview. The cops were shouting at the people behind the barricades, trying their best to keep them contained.

The two-minute walk from the car to the courthouse seemed like eternity, my adrenaline running high from all of the noise and the people.

Officers were all over in the courthouse as well. After I was searched and walked through the metal detector, I met up with my attorney, who had been in the courthouse since the very minute it opened that morning. Mr. Manny Sawyer, my lawyer, that had been fully paid for on behalf of Black Lives Matter. He was a tall guy, shiny white teeth, and built like a cop. Well, he tried to run me through what to do during the trial but I arrived too late.

All he said was, don't say anything. I got this. I'm going to get you home, baby boy."

I had only been in the courthouse for 10 minutes and I could feel the manipulation in the air. All of the corruption, all of the people framed for crimes they have never done. The place reeked of injustice and moral indecency. The judges and lawyers are the masters of hypocrisy, throwing people's lives away, all while committing the same crimes on a higher level. Pointing at the stick in everyone else's eye, meanwhile, they have a log in their ass. Systematic oppression, modern-day slavery. The real soldiers of Iraq are the men in white and black. The butterflies ran wild in my stomach; the pressure was getting to me.

I walked into the courtroom with my lawyer on my right side. A white man was standing by a wooden podium with a nice, all gray tuxedo. He looked really sharp, then I realized he was the prosecutor. That man was the enemy and just like the devil, he is the one dressed like a good man. My lawyer looked at me when we got by our podium with a confident look. To me, his body language assured me that he would fight until he couldn't go anymore.

There was an all-white jury, which made me uncertain but people have won in the past with a white jury. I also already expected that from the start. There were a lot of people in the stands, watching the trial. I'm just happy there are no cameras in here. The judge walked in from a back entrance with an all-black gown. A tall Hispanic man, his name is Judge Moore, also known as "More Time Moore." His plan was to give out a million years before he passed away. Just my luck.

"All rise," said the bailiff. "Judge Moore presiding."

"You all may be seated," said Judge Moore. The show has started. "This is case number 18799-244, the State of North Dakota vs. Jamari Picard. Mr. Picard has been charged with aggravated assault on Mr. Freddy Willis."

After the introduction, the District Attorney started by saying that I attacked Mr. Willis after class because I was trying to kill him for his girlfriend, Laurie. The attorney also mentioned that he had 2 witnesses that saw the whole thing and 3 statements. He also said that Laurie has run away from home because of me. The demon in the grey suit's job was to make me the property of the state and was willing to say anything to threaten my freedom.

While he was saying all of this, I got nervous and started tapping my foot, and I noticed he started choking on his words. Then I remembered what Mrs. Swiswi gave me.

The D.A. paused and began speaking again. "Mr. Picard has a known track record of... of... of..." I tapped my foot and stopped him right in his tracks. Oh shit, this really works, thank God.

Now it was time for my lawyer to speak. "Mr. Picard is 17 years old and has been an honors student since kindergarten. He lived in Miami, Florida all his life up until he moved here to Williston. In the school Mr. Picard attends, there are only 4 people of color, which makes him outcast in the school. He will be graduating high school in 2 months, your honor. Mr. Picard has no reason to assault this young man. He was simply defending himself.

"When Mr. Willis found out Jamari left a party with Ms. Laurie, a party which another one of their peers was throwing, he became angry and plotted revenge on Mr. Picard, after he became aware of the light romance between Mr. Picard and Ms. Laurie. The new black kid had sex with his girl and he did not take that lightly. That's why he attacked Mr. Picard at school."

Damn, my lawyer was good but I don't think that would be enough to win this trial. The people in the stands looked completely outraged by what Mr. Sawyer said. Meanwhile, the jury seemed unconvinced.

The D.A. started up again. "Mr. Willis is still wearing metal wiring in his mouth. The boy was on his way to class like any other student when he was struck by the defendant. Mr. Picard was on drugs that morning, the same as when he left the party with Ms. Laurie. Self-defense is protecting yourself but witnesses at the scene claim that Mr. Picard bashed Mr. Willis' face in, also, not to mention in all of the history of Williston High School, there has not been one fight until Mr. Picard began going to the school."

What the fuck? all of that was complete bullshit. How could he possibly know if I was high or not? And that fucking redneck hit me first. It was recess time and my attorney advised me to keep calm and maintain good body language. He bought a bag of nacho chips from the vending machine and a grape soda.

After that quick snack, it was back on stage. We walked in the courtroom and the people in the stands started sobbing loudly. It was as if they were purposely trying to get the judge's attention. Fuck. This is looking bad.

The judge ordered them to calm down or they will be thrown out, so they calmed down.

The D.A. began again. "So, let's hear from witness 1."

Then the first witness took the stand. His name is Corey Edwards. A short, blond hair kid that went to my school. He is apparently Freddy's best friend. "I walked out of class because the bell rang, and I met up with Freddy. As we were walking through the hallway, I noticed Jamari from afar, watching... I noticed... Ja... Ja... I... I... I..." He started stuttering, then he froze up and couldn't speak much. Every time he paused and tried to resume where he left off, I would tap my foot. I couldn't let this asshole speak, he will try to get me buried 1 mile under the courthouse. Corey started crying and was asked to leave the stand because he seemed frightened and shook up by the whole situation. Then another witness was called to the stand.

Steve Wentz. I looked at him so surprised. I never expected him to take the stand on me. I did not think he was a snitch. He seemed like too much of a stoner to do that police shit. Steve got on the stand and looked at me with a regretful face. I already knew to expect the worst from him. After all, he did not owe me anything. He barely even knows me for the most part.

"Ah, that guy sitting right there," Steve said while pointing at me, "was at my party and then he left with Laurie. Then about a week later, I saw him, and..." I tapped my foot hard as hell. The guy Steve at least confirmed my lawyer's story but I didn't know what else he is going to say, so I couldn't let him speak anymore. I gave him the benefit of the doubt, at least.

Mr. Sawyer, "On the day of Picard's arrest, while he was in custody, he was taken into the infirmary where he was evaluated, and the doctors made a note of an injury to the back of his head. The same place where Mr. Willis struck my client. Now, Mr. Willis also has a record of lawbreaking behavior, according to the state files. Mr. Willis has been to 3 juvenile programs on charges from armed carjacking to hunting with an unauthorized weapon. This man Freddy Willis is no saint. He is indeed a trouble maker. My client defended himself when he was attacked by the violent Freddy Willis."

During the whole thing, I was thinking about the fight I had with the guy. It's unfortunate for something so small to be blown up into such a big deal. Hopefully, my attorney's final argument was enough to save my ass because I drop the soap sometimes at home.

I scanned the room in search of Keylina. Still, she has yet to appear. Her beautiful smile and shiny long black hair were to die for. She comes from a rich Latin, Native American family and embraces her culture wholeheartedly.

Things suddenly became less about me and more about her. I was too far in love to go to prison. The first time I get the taste of happiness in my mouth, the world tries to force something bitter down my throat.

The judge called another recess to give the jury time to deliberate. Since I asked for a speedy trial, everything was to be handled today.

I checked the clock and it was 11:10 and we had to return at 12:30. My attorney looked at me very confident but I was feeling thoughtful. Keylina has my child in her stomach, man. Being in prison won't help me raise that kid. I also don't want to leave her in that position. To be a single mother raising a child at 18. I would screw her life up. It would be horrible to be doing time with that kind of pressure on my chest. I can't do it, no sir, not me. I refuse to go to prison.

The clock was speeding, man. It's already time for the verdict. Shit man! My stomach was bubbling like simmering water. The shit in my ass was about to come out. I have to squeeze my cheeks as hard as possible for the shit not to slip out. My heart started beating like a woodpecker pecking on wood. I felt like I was being drilled with an electric drill in my chest.

I started taking baby steps back into the courtroom, trying my best to prolong my fate but I had no choice; "ain't no turning around" like Yo Gotti said. I sat down in my leather rolling chair, shaking like a wet dog. I was very anxious. My adrenaline was pumping, something had to give.

The judge walked in, we all rose and sat down like we hadn't seen him earlier today. The evidence table had a few stacks of paper and video clips from school but they didn't have any real evidence. The best they had was Steve Wentz and he confirmed my lawyer's story. Let's see what happens.

Freddy Willis' family was sobbing in the stands, loud but not disturbing. It was surely loud enough for me to feel like I was going to be found guilty.

The judge looked up and said, "Where is the jury's representative?" Then a young guy with curly hair stepped up and looked around like an owl. He surveyed the whole room.

At that very moment, the place was mute. You could hear two officers in the back room betting a night out to drink if I was found guilty.

The guy had to be in his late 20's. He stood tall and firm. He took a deep breath and said, "The jury finds Jamari Picard not guilty on the count of aggravated assault." The earth shook. I had a mental avalanche. I could not believe it, I'm not guilty; I'm free. They saw I was only defending myself. A big weight was lifted off my shoulders.

Mr. Sawyer, on the other hand, seemed unbothered by the decision. The judge looked at me as if he was confused but still, he grabbed his gavel, then he said, "Jamari Picard, not guilty," reluctantly.

The Willis family erupted like a volcano. I don't know if that lady was his mom or what but she fell out on the floor. The people in the stands all stood up, outraged like their home basketball team lost in overtime with a close buzzer-beater shot.

Mr. Sawyer took me and told me to get up and go. He rushed me out of the courtroom. As soon as we got outside the courtroom, he did the famous air punch professional baseball pitchers do after a strikeout. He was excited, man. He also told me that this was half the battle. The real war was on the outside. Mr. Sawyer grabbed my face, then said, "Kid, when you walk out the double doors, you will get the hell out of North Dakota as soon as possible. They will kill you for that white boy. A black does not get away with stuff like that!" All of that shit Mr. Sawyer was saying did not matter to me. I'm not going to prison.

"I truly appreciate your services, Mr. Sawyer, but listen here. You and I both know that I was a publicity stunt to raise your paralegal status and for Black Lives Matter to get more donation money. You people steal off the money that should be used to empower our people. You are no different than that demon in the grey suit. People like you are the reason why our people are the way they are now, so please, Mr. Sawyer, let me go my way," I said as most polite and respectful as possible.

Mr. Sawyer still looked like he wanted to fight but instead, he put his hands on his waist, looked around, and walked me to the exit. He was speechless that a 17-year-old boy knew the secret he was hiding. I knew what his card was. I read his poker face. Mr. Sawyer is nothing but a servant boy of the white man and I know it.

We walked out of the building and the crowd of people was everywhere. I froze up at first when I saw the mass amount of people. Cameras were flashing and journalists everywhere with microphones reaching towards me.

The policemen were the only ones stopping me from getting ambushed by the people looking for the once in a lifetime story that would start their career of reporting and violating the lives of people at the expense of a paycheck. These people go through this just so an average Joe could drink his coffee with some entertainment.

"Mr. Picard, what do you have to say?" "What's the verdict?" How do you feel, Mr. Picard?"

The last question struck my ear with force. I turned my neck to the beautiful journalist and said, "I feel great. The powers of colonialism was defeated today. My win today is one of the few. I hope that I can serve as a message to all my brothers and sisters, people of color, Asians, Latinos, Indian, white, black, brown, yellow, and red. That no matter what type of situation, no matter what the condition, you must fight. Never give up, never lose hope. Keep ya head up, like Tupac said." I don't know what took over me but I felt that was the right thing to do.

I walked into the car after the statement I made, feeling like I owned the universe.

As soon as I laid my eyes on Keylina, I told her I love her. We hugged and kissed like we hadn't seen each other in years. The car took off and all the thousands of people became a faded blur. They became another memory of the past. I was overwhelmed with joy. I also thanked Mrs. Swiswi for all of the support and the protection that saved me in the courtroom. I'm happy to be a part of this family. Speaking of family, I wonder if Keylina told her mother about the pregnancy but that doesn't matter now. We must celebrate this victory. I was liberated, just when I was supposed to enter the mouth of the lion.

"Keylina, I love you. And thank you, Mrs. Swiswi." "Love you too, Jamari."

"You're welcome, son." "Where are we going now?"

"We are headed to one of the chiefs in Fargo's home to give thanks to the ancestors."

"Is there going to be food, mom?"

"Of course, there will be plenty of food."

On the highway, excited to be leaving Williston a free man. I almost became a victim of the justice system that has been destroying the lives of people for hundreds of years. Thank God I made it out. Being on the road with Keylina made me think about how much she meant to me. I really love this girl and I almost had to surrender her to go to prison. I promise I will never abandon her as long as I'm on this earth. Staring out of the window and seeing the snow and the fire coming from the oil rigs made me also think about how long I been on this journey. I came to think, now this is my home, I got a beautiful girl, I don't need anything else. As we were on the road, the words not guilty was echoing in my head. It's scary to know that people want me in prison and because of the fact, I'm vindicated. I'm a target now.

Wondering what the news headlines are now. Laugh my ass off. I don't give a fuck, I'm on the highway to heaven. Feeling like Snoop Dogg when he beat that case. Nothing can stop me now!

I fell asleep and I woke up an hour later. We were still on the road. This trip seems to be taking forever. Keylina was asleep too, like the angel she is, leaning on the car window. I looked over to Mrs. Swiswi and she seemed worried for some reason. She kept looking at the rearview mirrors. Then I glanced at the dash and saw she was going 100 miles per hour. That's well over 40 miles above the speed limit. Then Bam! the car was hit from the back! and the car went spinning on the freeway. Keylina woke up, then her side of the vehicle slammed straight into the wall.

The car felt like it was spinning for an hour. Everything happened fast but it felt so long. Smoke was coming from the hood of the car. The windshield was cracked. Mrs. Swiswi's head was on the steering wheel, looking lifeless. Keylina was bleeding from her forehead. I was trying to move but I couldn't; my body was too heavy. I felt like I'm high or something. My vision is blurry.

Although I love Keylina and care for her, my only concern was trying to save myself. I was staring at the car door but my arm was stuck. Suddenly, the car door was opened and a man with a grey tuxedo and black shoes looked at me. Then he drew an all-black 9mm handgun and pointed it to my head. I was too hurt to feel scared. My mind was gone. The only thing I knew was, I had seen that grey suit before, then it touched me; that's the District Attorney. He came to end my life. That was his mission one way or another, he was going to kill me. At least I won the first battle, the war will be fought...

"Guilty, Jamari Picard. The jury finds you guilty." Then Bam! he let off the pistol. The last thing I saw was the flame from the chamber. The only thing I was guilty of was being black in America.

Chapter 20

I woke up from my daydream when the cries of an infant overthrew the room as the judge slammed the gavel. "The State of North Dakota finds Jamari Picand guilty of Manslaughter for the death of Freddy Willis." My heart sank like the Titanic. All of my dreams and everything I ever knew was destroyed. That blow was too hard for me to chew. The only person that seemed to feel as bad as I do was that baby crying. I looked around and I saw Laurie holding a baby in her hand. The baby was not going to stop crying, so Laurie got up and left. Seeing her made me frustrated. She is the reason I'm in this position now. I sat in the county jail for a year now and I have not heard from her, not one single time. I'm facing a life sentence because of her. She had a psycho boyfriend; they attacked me. It's not my fault that when I slammed him he landed on his neck and died. He should have never run up on me. If I could kill somebody right now, it would be her. Now my life will never have any meaning. I'm just another person added to the overpopulated prison system. I'm nothing but a hustle so the government can get more funding.

I wonder... My lawyer did not have any type of emotion on his face. The judge's decision does not seem to bother him, not one bit. I may spend the rest of my life in prison and he will still make the same weekly salary. I don't mean anything to him and I never will. As much as I want to hurt this idiot, I can't. The only statement my attorney made to me was that he will appeal the judge's decision but Lord knows how many years will pass before I get a response. I might as well give up on everything that I know out there. Keylina and I will never be together. I will never become the well-known artist I wanted to be. I will never be with my family again. All hope is lost.

I might be spending the rest of my life in prison because of a girl; how stupid is that?

Freddy Willis's family were celebrating the judge's decision, and yes, they were emotional. Tears and plenty of screams during the trial. Sad that two lives had to be stolen from the world because of one tragic situation.

The guard came to my side of the courtroom to escort me back to the holding cell. I stood up with shackles on my feet and the guard put cuffs on my hands. The cuffs were cold, it made me get goosebumps. I feel down; my knees were too weak. I could not assemble the strength to keep going. Two officers came running to me to help me up.

The room quickly got into an uproar. Freddy Willis's mom yelled, "I hope you die!" Sadly, she doesn't know that I too wish I was a friend of death right now.

The officers carried me to the holding cell, where I sobbed at the realization I'm facing the maximum of life imprisonment. 10/10 times, when someone goes to trial for murder and they lose, they get life. Why God? Why? Take me with you. I can't spend the rest of my life behind bars.

I started to feel pains in my stomach, I felt like a Harley Davidson. For the next hour, I was confined in a small cold room until they figured I got better. I did not feel any better, but I had to man up; I can't go back to the dorm crying. Those dudes will make me their bitch before I wipe my face.

The officer looked at me with his keys in hand and said, "Kid, you don't deserve this. You should be in school." I nodded my head to embarrass the deputy. He was right. That's where I got arrested. I haven't seen anyone since that day. My family gave up on me. Everyone and everything I know was an illusion, all fake and phony. The only thing I can look forward to is the afterlife. I may be happy then.

When I got back to the dorm, it was the same shit. Guys playing cards and dominoes in orange jumpsuits. Black on the right, whites on the left, and Mexicans in their corner. Some guys were smoking in the back by the showers. The only time when the races mixed together was at the phones and the gambling table.

The only thing I wanted to do was sleep. I felt sicker than someone with heroin withdrawals. I entered the room and all eyes shifted towards me. Someone yelled out, "You will be alright, Baby Boy." My head was faced on the floor. I did not even look to see who said that.

The officer removed my restraints and handed me a tray of food. A hot dog with baked beans and a slice of bread. That was one of the best meals in this place but I said fuck that shit. I took it in my cell and left it on the counter. I climbed up and laid in my bunk, then my cellmate entered the room. "Jamari, I know you're feeling down right now but you're all over the news. The street is going crazy. You will have a good fighting chance on appeal, don't sweat it."

"I'll come out in a little bit."

"Them Aryan Nation boys mad as hell you all over the TV People all over the county protesting."

That did not surprise me; those bigots hate me because I got the media eyes on the corrupt prison and justice system. Those guys are the dumbest motherfuckers on earth. They actually think they are a part of the ultimate race. Fucking idiots.

Damn man, I lost; I'm going to do life. I cried quietly under my sheets until a deep slumber took me. When I woke up, it was count time. I stood up for the count, thinking Damn, every day for the rest of my life I will be standing at 4:00, 10:00, and 7:00 for the count. I can't do this shit.

I got into my bed after count cleared, my cellmate went to exercise. I laid on my bunk, depressed. Then I felt a cold chill run down my spine. The room was too cold for sleep right now, so I got up to go use the phone.

When I walked out of my cell, two Aryan Brotherhood dudes were outside of my cell but I didn't see them, my head was down. They approached me from behind when I walked past them. I felt a deep pain in my torso. I already knew what was happening but I did not fight it. The two guys ambushed me and filled me up with holes all over my body. The most painful one was the first one. All the rest did not have any feeling. Two white guys that prayed to a photo of Hitler stabbed me at least 40 times. They had tattoos all over their body and had the famous swastika tattooed on their face. I tried to cover my wounds but I had too many to cover.

As I laid on the floor, a war broke out; whites vs. blacks. These two guys went on to stab another guy but he had his knife on him. He fought back and killed one of the dudes.

The whole dorm was on lockdown. I was the first person lying on the floor but I wasn't the only one. My vision became blurry after 5 minutes. All I could see was blood covering the floor around me and guys fighting and running for their life. Chaos. Complete chaos. "Wake up! Wake up!" was the only thing I could hear. It sounded like Jamal's voice to me.

The officers came in and pepper-sprayed and shot people with bean bags until everything was done.

Epilogue

7 men died and 22 people placed in the hole. The biggest riot to occur in Williston County Jail history. Following the death of Jamari, a series of events took place. His hometown of Miami, Florida burned down over 3 miles of buildings in the downtown area. The damages were over a billion dollars. Other cities like Chicago had riots and protests that lasted weeks. The President of the United States declared a state of emergency and the National Guard had to step in. Donald Trump called people black extremists. Meanwhile, in predominantly white neighborhoods, the death of Jamari Picand was celebrated.

The child Laurie held in her hands turned out to be the son of Jamari. She named him Jamari Jr. in honor of his father. Ms. Laurie moved away from North Dakota and ended up in California, marrying a well-educated black man. They had 3 kids together and are doing fine.

Keylina moved back to her hometown after she graduated high school. She enrolled in college for business and got a job as a CEO of a small start-up company.

Jamesha divorced her husband after he molested his son one day, after getting drunk. The whole time he was abusing her and the kids.

Freddy Willis's family is one of the wealthiest families in North Dakota. Billie Willis, Freddy's father, owned over a hundred oil rigs in the state. He is a billionaire with a lot of power, knowing people in very high places.

Steve Wentz died 2 weeks after Jamari's death. He tried meth for the first time and overdosed.

Carmena's death was a suicide but one of the boys in the video was identified and was taken into custody for questioning, where he admitted to placing drugs in her drink. He cooperated with the police and 5 other guys got indicted by the Florida grand jury.

Jamari's mother became an activist following his death. She speaks at schools and encourages the youth to vote and live a drug-free lifestyle.

One year after Jamari's death, President Donald Trump passed a bipartisan deal for blacks to be judged by a black judge and have a jury of all black peers to fight the injustice in the system. He also passed a prison reform bill for all people that have been incarcerated for their first offense for over 10 years to be summarily released. They also passed on even task force law stating only a man living in a neighborhood can become a police officer in that area to stop racial profiling.

Every city in the United States has renamed a street in their city to Picard Street in the memory of Jamari. His death changed the nation as a whole. Every March 28 is Picard Day, a holiday in the name of the one that changed the world.

It is easy to sleep but it is hard to see the shadow behind the dream.

www.ingramcontent.com/pod-product-compliance
Lightning Source LLC
Chambersburg PA
CBHW081919130726
47909CB00015B/3029